Scarlet Wilson wrote her first story aged eight and has never stopped. She's worked in the health service for twenty years, trained as a nurse and a health visitor. Scarlet now works in public health and lives on the West Coast of Scotland with her fiancé and their two sons. Writing medical romances and contemporary romances is a dream come true for her.

Also by Scarlet Wilson

Christmas with the Maverick Millionaire
The Doctor She Left Behind
A Touch of Christmas Magic
The Doctor's Baby Secret
A Baby to Save Their Marriage
One Kiss in Tokyo…
Christmas in the Boss's Castle
A Royal Baby for Christmas
The Doctor and the Princess
The Mysterious Italian Houseguest

Discover more at millsandboon.co.uk.

A FAMILY MADE AT CHRISTMAS

SCARLET WILSON

MILLS & BOON

First published in Great Britain 2017
by Mills & Boon, an imprint of HarperCollins*Publishers*
1 London Bridge Street, London, SE1 9GF

Large Print edition 2018

© 2017 Scarlet Wilson

ISBN: 978-0-263-07275-4

This book is produced from independently certified
FSC™ paper to ensure responsible forest management. For
more information visit www.harpercollins.co.uk/green.

Printed and bound in Great Britain
by CPI Group (UK) Ltd, Croydon, CR0 4YY

This book is dedicated to Sheila Hodgson, my fabulous editor. Thank you for believing in this story and letting me see it through, and thank you for being the best advocate for Medical Romance in the world!

CHAPTER ONE

'HURRY UP, RILEY. It's your round.' The hard slap on the shoulder nearly ejected him from his chair. Riley laughed and turned around. Frank Cairney, one of the rehab nurses, was standing with his rucksack on his shoulder. The rest of the team were hovering outside near the door. 'Should I go and hold up the bar for us?'

Riley nodded. 'Just a few notes to finish and I'll be there. Thanks, guys.'

He typed quickly on the electronic record, leaving detailed notes on the plan for Jake Ashford, a soldier injured on duty in Afghanistan and now a resident in the army rehab hospital at Waterloo Court.

It was late afternoon on a Friday. Those who could go home had gone home. But some patients wouldn't be able to go home for some time—Jake was one of those.

Working in the rehab hospital hadn't really

been on Riley's career plan. But, due to a family crisis, a fellow colleague hadn't been able to start when he should have, meaning the hospital needed someone to fill in. Riley's surgical experience in orthopaedics had been flagged and his deployment had been delayed on a temporary basis for a few weeks.

But today was his last shift. And truth was he was relieved. The staff and support team at Waterloo Court were fantastic, as were the world-class rehab services, but Riley liked the pace of emergencies. On Monday he'd be in Sierra Leone, where another outbreak of Ebola seemed to be emerging.

He finished his notes and walked down the corridor to the in-patient beds. He heard the laughter before he saw her familiar frame.

April Henderson had Jake sitting at the side of his bed. Laughing. Really laughing, as if she'd just told him the funniest joke in the world.

Even from here he knew exactly what she was doing—testing Jake's sitting balance. She was one of the best physiotherapists he'd ever worked with.

She was tireless. She was relentless. She was polite. She was professional.

He'd caught himself on more than one occasion watching that blonde ponytail swishing up the corridor in front of him as she made her way between the ninety patients that were housed in the state-of-the-art unit.

But even now—four weeks later—he really didn't know a thing about her.

April was the quietest co-worker he'd ever met. Every conversation, every communication had been about their patients. When he asked her about life, what she was doing at the weekend or anything other than work she just shut down.

He'd asked other staff a few questions about her, but no one really said much. Apparently she wasn't married and hadn't mentioned a boyfriend. The staff here were a mixture of military and civilian. April was civilian. She'd transferred to the new unit at Waterloo Court. The centre dealt with serious musculoskeletal injuries, neurological injuries and complex trauma, including amputees. The brand-new facility was four times bigger than its predecessor. There were gyms, full of cardiovascular and resistance equipment, two swimming pools, a hydrotherapy pool and a specialist centre where artificial limbs were manufactured on-site and individually tailored to the patients' needs.

'Doc?' Jake caught his eye.

Riley crossed the room, holding out his hand. 'I came to say goodbye.' He paused for a second. 'I'm shipping out again tomorrow.' He had to be truthful, but he could see the momentary pang in the young man's eyes. Jake loved the army. Had wanted to serve since he was five. And now, at the grand old age of twenty-three, would be unlikely to ever ship out again.

Jake took Riley's extended hand. 'Good luck, Doc—it's been short and sweet. Where are you headed?'

Riley gave a shrug. 'At the moment, I think it's Africa. But you know how things can change. By the time Monday comes around it could be somewhere else completely.'

He glanced down at April, who was leaning against a stool at the side of the bed. 'Are you coming to the farewell drinks, April?'

It was obvious he'd caught her off guard because two tiny pink spots flared in her cheeks and she stumbled over her words. 'Wh-what? Er…no…sorry. I don't think I'll manage.'

Jake nudged her with one of his dangling feet. 'Oh, go on, April. When was the last time you could tell me a good night out story?'

The pinkness spread. But the shy demeanour vanished instantly. He'd always found that curious about her. April Henderson knew how to engage with her patients. *Really* engage with her patients. Around them she was relaxed, open and even showed the occasional glimmer of fun. But around any of the staff? She was just April.

'I'm not here to tell you night out stories, Jake. I'm here to help get you back on your feet again.' She leaned forward and put her hands on his bare leg. 'But don't think I didn't notice that deliberate kick.' She looked up and gave Jake a wide smile. 'That's great. That's something we can work on.'

With her bright blue eyes, blonde hair and clear skin, April Henderson could be stunning if she wanted to be. But there was never any make-up on her skin, never any new style with her hair. It was almost as if she used her uniform as a shield.

Riley watched the look on Jake's face. For the first time in weeks he saw something that hadn't been there much before. Hope.

It did weird things to his insides. Jake was a

young man who should be filled with hope. His whole life was ahead of him. But there was already a good hint that his injury could be limiting. They still didn't have a clear prognosis for him, and that was why April's work was so vital.

He winked at Jake and folded his arms across his chest. 'I'm completely and utterly offended that you won't come to my farewell drinks. Four long weeks here, all those shifts together, and you can't even say goodbye.'

'He's right, April.' Jake nodded. 'It is shocking. Thank goodness you're not actually in the army. At this point you'd be getting a dishonourable discharge.'

For the briefest of seconds there was a flash of panic behind her eyes, quickly followed by the realisation that they were kidding with her.

She raised her eyebrows. Gave her best smile. The one reserved for patients in trouble. Both of them recognised it instantly.

'Uh-oh,' Riley muttered.

April touched Jake's leg. 'Well, just so you know, Jake, now that we've established there's some movement and—' she stood up '—your balance is gradually improving, I think I'll have a whole new plan for you, starting tomorrow.'

Jake groaned as Riley laughed. He couldn't quite work out why April could chat easily with patients but could barely say a word to him on a normal day.

Jake pointed at Riley. 'This is all your fault. You're abandoning me to this wicked, wicked woman. You know she'll work me hard and exhaust me.' He said the words with a twinkle in his eyes.

Riley nodded as he glanced at April. Her blue gaze met his. For the first time since he'd met her, she didn't look away instantly. He smiled. 'You're right, Jake. But I'm leaving you with one of the best physios I've ever met. She'll push you to your absolute limit—exactly what you need. If anyone can get you back on your feet again, it's April Henderson.' He put his hand on Jake's shoulder as he leaned forward to fake whisper in his ear, 'Even if she won't have a drink with me.'

There was something about that bright blue gaze. Even under the harsh hospital lights that seemed to drain the colour from everyone else, April still looked good. The edges of her mouth gave just the slightest hint of turning upwards. It was the first time he'd wished he wasn't leaving.

Jake reached up and grabbed his hand, giving it a shake. 'Thanks, Lieutenant Callaghan. Good luck with your deployment.' There was a tiny waver in his voice. Almost as if he knew the likelihood was he'd never make another deployment himself.

Riley clasped his hand between his. 'I'll look you up again when I come back.' He started towards the door, then glanced over his shoulder and gave a warm smile. 'You too, April.'

Her heart was acting as though she were racing along a beach, rather than sitting at the side of a patient's bed.

Darn it.

Ever since Riley Callaghan had turned up on this ward she'd spent the last four weeks avoiding him. It was everything. The little kink in his dark hair. The smiling green eyes. The cheeky charm. Oh, lots of doctors and servicemen she'd met in the last few years had the talk, the wit, the *lots* of charm.

But she'd had enough to deal with. The diagnosis of her twin sister's ovarian cancer, rapidly followed by her failing treatment, then Mallory's death, had meant that she had found it easier to retreat into herself and seal herself off from the world. Her own genetic testing had floored her. She had decisions to make. Plans for the future.

Her last relationship had been half-hearted. Mallory had got sick and she'd realised quickly that she needed to spend time with her sister. But, since then, the last thing she wanted was a relationship.

After her own testing, she'd spent a day wondering whether she should just find some random guy, try to get pregnant, have a baby quickly and deal with everything else after.

But those thoughts had only lasted a day. She'd met the surgeon. A date for her surgery would be agreed soon. And she needed to do this part of her life alone.

Then Riley Callaghan had appeared on her ward. All cheeky grins and twinkling eyes. It was the first time in a long time she'd actually been aware of every sense in her body. Her surge of adrenaline. Every rapid heartbeat.

That was the reason she didn't engage in small

talk. That was the reason she kept to herself. She couldn't afford to let herself be attracted to a guy at such a crucial point in her life. How did you start that conversation anyway? Oh, you want to go on a date? Great. By the way, in a few months' time I'm going to have my ovaries and fallopian tubes removed and maybe later my breasts. What? You don't want to hang around?

It didn't matter that she'd found herself glancing in Riley's direction every time he'd appeared on the ward. She'd hated the way she'd started stumbling over her words around him, or had trouble looking him in the eye.

But as she watched his retreating back her mouth felt dry. Part of her wanted to grab her jacket and join the rest of the staff for a drink. But then she'd be in a pub, where her inhibitions could lower, and she could encourage the gentle flirtation that could go absolutely nowhere.

She shook her head and turned her attention back to Jake. 'Can we get you more comfortable? I'll work on your new programme and we'll start tomorrow.'

Jake gave her a nod and she helped settle him in

a comfortable, specially designed chair for those with spinal injuries.

Her shift was finished but it wouldn't take long to write up her notes and make the adjustments needed for tomorrow. It wasn't as if she had anywhere to go, right?

Half an hour later there were a few voices in the corridor behind her. This was a military hospital. When the Colonel appeared, it was never good news.

All the hairs bristled on her arms. She looked around, wondering who was about to get bad news.

'Ms Henderson?'

She spun around in her chair and jumped to her feet. Her? How? What?

A woman with a pinched face and dark grey coat stood next to the Colonel. She didn't even know that he knew her name.

'Y-yes,' she stumbled.

'We're wondering where Lieutenant Callaghan is.'

Her heart plummeted in her chest. Riley? They had bad news for Riley?

She glanced around. 'He's not here. But I know

where he is. Can you give me five minutes? I'll get him for you.'

The Colonel nodded and she rushed past, going to the changing room and grabbing her jacket. If she ran, the pub was only five minutes away.

As soon as she stepped outside she realised just how much the temperature had dipped. It was freezing and it was only the middle of November. As she thudded down the dark path a few snowflakes landed on her cheeks. Snow? Already?

She slowed her run. If spots of rain had turned to snow, then there was a chance the damp ground would be slippery.

The pub came into view, warm light spilling from its windows. She stopped running completely, her warm breath steaming in the air around her.

She could hear the noise and laughter coming from the pub already. She closed her eyes for a second. She hated that she was about to do this. To walk into a farewell party and pull Riley away for news he probably wouldn't want. Did his family serve in the military? Did he have a brother? She just didn't know. She hadn't allowed herself to have that kind of conversation with Riley.

She pushed open the door to the pub, the heat hitting her instantly. It was busy. She jostled her way through the people, scanning one way then another. It didn't take long to recognise the laugh. She picked Riley's familiar frame out of the crowd and pushed herself towards him. Her work colleagues were picking up glasses and toasting him. She stumbled as she reached him, her hands coming out and landing square on his chest. His hard, muscular chest.

'April?' He looked completely surprised. 'Oh, wow. You made it. That's great.' His arm had automatically gone around her shoulder. He pulled her a little closer to try to talk above the noise in the pub. 'Can I get you something to drink?'

He frowned as he noticed she hadn't even changed out of her uniform.

She looked up into his green eyes. 'Riley, I'm sorry—I'm not here for the drinks.'

He pulled back a little whilst keeping his arm on her shoulder. 'You aren't?'

Her hands were still on his chest. She really didn't want to move them. 'Riley—' she pressed her lips together for a second '—the Colonel is looking for you. He came to the ward.'

She felt every part of his body tense.

'What?' His voice had changed.

She nodded. 'I said I'd come and get you.'

Riley didn't even say goodbye to anyone around him. He just grabbed hold of her hand and pulled her behind him as he jostled his way through the crowd.

The snow was falling as they reached the main door. Riley spun around to face her, worry etched all over his face. 'What did he say? Is it just the Colonel?'

April shook her head. 'He didn't tell me anything. And there's an older woman with him. I didn't recognise her.'

She reached up and touched his arm. It didn't matter that she'd vowed to keep a distance. This was a completely different set of circumstances. This was a work colleague who was likely to receive some bad news. She'd never leave a workmate alone at a time like this. 'Let me come back with you' was all she said.

And, after the longest few seconds, Riley gave a nod.

* * *

He started walking quickly but eventually just broke into a run. His brother. It had to be his brother. He was on a training exercise right now somewhere in Scotland, flying out to Afghanistan tomorrow. Accidents happened. As a doctor, he knew that more than most. Unless something had happened to his mum and dad. Could they have had an accident?

He was conscious of the footsteps beside him. The ones that broke into a gentle run when he did. He'd been surprised by April's appearance earlier—it had made his heart lurch for a few seconds. But it hadn't taken long to notice the paleness of her complexion. The worry in her bright blue eyes. And she was right by his side. Trouble was, right now he couldn't think straight.

By the time he reached the ward area his brain was spinning completely. He slowed down to a walk, took a few deep breaths and tried to put on his professional face. He was a soldier. He could deal with whatever news he was about to receive.

The Colonel ushered him into a room where a woman in a grey coat was sitting with a file in front of her.

April hovered near the door—she didn't seem to know whether to leave or not—and he was kind of glad she was still around.

'Lieutenant Callaghan. Please take a seat.'

He didn't want to sit. In fact, sitting was the last thing he wanted to do. But if it would get this thing over with quicker then he'd do it.

He sat down and glanced at the woman. She leaned across the table towards him. 'Dr Callaghan, my name is Elizabeth Cummings. I'm a social worker.'

He frowned. A social worker? Why did she need to speak to him?

She flicked open her file. 'I understand that this might seem a little unusual. Can I ask, do you know an Isabel Porter?'

He flinched. This was not what he'd been expecting to hear. He glanced at the Colonel. 'Sir, my parents? My brother?'

The Colonel shook his head and gestured back to Ms Cummings. 'No. They're fine. They're absolutely fine. Please, this is something else entirely.'

Riley shifted in his chair. He glanced behind at April. She looked just as confused as he was.

Now he felt uncomfortable. He looked back at the social worker. 'Isabel Porter, from Birmingham?'

The woman nodded.

'Yes, I know Isabel. At least, I did. Around five years ago. Why are you asking me that?'

Ms Cummings gave a nod. 'I see. Dr Callaghan, I'm sorry to tell you that there was an accident a few days ago. Isabel was killed in a road traffic accident.'

It was like a cold prickle down his spine. Nothing about this seemed right. 'Oh, I see. I'm really sorry to hear that. But I don't understand. Why are you telling me?' He looked from one tight face to the other.

Ms Cummings glanced at the Colonel. 'There is an issue we need to discuss. Ms Porter left a will.'

'Isabel had written a will?' Now that did sound weird. Isabel had been a bit chaotic. Their relationship had barely lasted a few months. And they hadn't kept in touch. He hadn't heard from her at all in the last five years. 'Why on earth are you telling me this?'

Ms Cummings slid an envelope across the desk

to him. 'Maybe this will help explain things.' She kept talking. 'Obviously there's been a delay. Isabel had no other family. No next of kin, which is probably why she left a will and wrote this letter for you. It takes time to find out if someone has left a will or not.'

Riley glanced at the letter on the table in front of him. He had no idea what was going on. Nothing about this made sense.

April walked over and put her hand on his shoulder. From the woman who'd seemed so shut off, it was such an unexpected move. But the warm feel of her palm on his shoulder sent a wave of pure comfort through his confused state.

Ms Cummings stared at April for a second then continued. 'It's apparent that your name wasn't on the birth certificate. I'm not quite sure why that was. But because Isabel didn't have you formally named as next of kin, Finn has been in temporary foster care for the last few days.'

Riley shook his head. 'Who?'

She stared at him. 'Finn. Your son.'

For the first time he was glad of the chair. If he hadn't had it, his legs might have made him sway.

'My son?'

Ms Cummings glanced at the Colonel again. 'Yes, Dr Callaghan. That's why I'm here.'

'I have a son?'

She stared at him again. 'Finn. He's five. Isabel never told you?'

He shook his head as his brain just spun. Not a single rational thought would form. 'No. Isabel never told me.'

Ms Cummings pushed the letter towards him again. He noticed it was sealed. The social worker had no idea of the contents. 'Well, maybe that's why she left you the letter.'

Riley looked at the cream envelope in front of him. He picked it up and ripped it open, pulling out a matching cream sheet of paper.

Dear Riley,

I hope you never have to read this. But if you do it's because something's happened. I'm sorry I never told you about Finn. You'd already left for Afghanistan and it just seemed pointless. We already knew our time was over and I didn't need to complicate your life.

I hope I'm not about to spoil things for you. I hope you've managed to meet someone, marry and have a family of your own.

Finn and I have been great. We haven't needed anything at all. He's a funny, quirky little boy and I can see traits of us both in him every single day. I love him more than you can ever know, and I hope you'll feel that way about him too.

He knows who you are. I only had a few pictures, but I put them in his room and told him you worked away and would meet him when he grew up.

Please forgive me, and love my darling boy for both of us.

Isabel

He couldn't speak. He couldn't breathe. His life had just been turned upside down and on its head. He had a child. He had a son.

And he'd never been told. Rage filled his brain, just as April's fingers tightened on his shoulder. She could probably read every word of the letter over his shoulder.

April leaned over and spun the letter around to face the social worker, giving her a few seconds to read it. Her face paled.

Ms Cummings looked at him. 'You didn't even know that Finn existed?'

He shook his head. The firm touch by April was dissipating the rage that was burning inside. Isabel had been quirky. She'd been a little chaotic. This didn't seem completely out of character. He just hadn't had a clue.

'Where is Finn now?' April's voice cut through his thoughts.

Ms Cummings looked up. 'And you are?'

April leaned across and held out her hand. 'I'm April Henderson. I'm a friend and colleague of Dr Callaghan's.' She said the words so easily. A friend. It almost sounded true.

Ms Cummings shuffled some papers. 'Finn's been in temporary foster care in Birmingham.'

Panic started to fill Riley. 'My son is in foster care?' He'd heard about these things. Wasn't foster care bad for kids?

Ms Cummings nodded. 'We have a few things to sort out. As your name isn't on the birth certificate, you may want to arrange a DNA test. However, Ms Porter named you as her son's guardian in her will. Pending a few checks, I'll be happy to release Finn into your custody. You will, of course, be allocated a local social worker to help you with any queries.' She lifted something from her bag. 'As you'll know, in England we have a number of legal procedures. Isabel left everything in trust—via you—for Finn. But probate takes some time. I can only let you have these keys to the house for a day or so—to pick some things up for Finn. Although ultimately it will come to you, the keys have to be returned to the lawyer in the meantime.'

'When do I pick up Finn?'

'Do you have somewhere suitable for him to stay?'

His thoughts went immediately to his temporary army lodgings. He was only supposed to be here four weeks. 'I'm supposed to leave for Sierra Leone on Monday.' The words came out of nowhere.

The Colonel interjected quickly. 'Don't worry. I'll take care of that. You have a family emergency. Your son obviously takes priority here. Do you want me to arrange some other accommodation for you?'

He nodded automatically. He didn't own a property. He had money in the bank but had never got around to buying a place as he'd no idea where he'd eventually end up.

His eyes caught sight of a box in the corner of the room. Red tinsel. It was stuffed full of Christmas decorations. Christmas. It was only six weeks away. His son had lost his mother, six weeks before Christmas.

'I'll give you an address. I can meet you at the foster parents' house tomorrow if that suits.'

'It suits.' The words were automatic.

Ms Cummings gave a nod. 'There's one other thing.'

'What's that?'

She licked her lips. 'As Ms Porter had no other next of kin and you're the only person named in the will, it will be up to you to organise the funeral.'

'What?'

Ms Cummings's eyes narrowed. 'Will that be a problem?'

He shook his head. 'No. Of course not.'

Ms Cummings pushed some papers towards him. 'Here's a copy of the will. A note of Ms Porter's address and her lawyer's address to drop the keys back. And a copy of the address for the foster family tomorrow. Let's say eleven o'clock?'

Business obviously concluded, she gathered

her papers and stood up. Riley glanced at the clock. In the space of ten minutes his life had just turned on its head.

'Do you have a picture?'

She looked startled. 'Of Finn?'

He nodded. Of course of Finn. Who did she think he wanted to see a picture of?

She reopened her file and slid out a small photograph. His mouth dried instantly. It was like a blast from the past. That small innocent face. Thirty years ago that had been him. A whole world he didn't even know existed.

He didn't even speak as the Colonel showed Ms Cummings out.

April had an ache deep inside her belly. This was a whole new Riley Callaghan in front of her right now.

He looked almost broken. She'd spent the last four weeks secretly watching his cheeky grin, positive interactions and boundless energy. There had been a few emergencies on the ward and Riley thought and moved quicker than anyone. He was a great doctor. Happy to help others. And always itching to get on to the next thing.

It was the first time she'd ever seen him slumped. He just seemed stunned.

His hand reached up and crumpled the letter on the table in front of him. She moved instinctively, brushing her fingers against his, pulling the paper from his and smoothing the paper back down.

'Don't. In a few years' time you might want to show that to Finn.'

He stood up so quickly the chair flew back and hit the floor. 'She didn't tell me. She didn't tell me about him.' He flung his hands up. 'How could she do that to me? How could she do that to him?'

April's mouth dried. She didn't know what to say. How on earth could she answer that question?

He started pacing, running his hands through his thick dark hair. 'What do I do? I don't know the first thing about children. I don't know how to be a father. What if he doesn't like me? What if I suck at being a dad?' He threw his hands out again. 'I don't have a house. What do I buy for a five-year-old? What does a five-year-old boy need? And what about my job? Will I still work here? What about school? Does Finn even go to school yet? I move about, all over the place. How can that be good for a kid?'

April took a deep breath. It was clear that every thought in his brain was just tumbling straight out of his mouth. She shook her head and stood in front of him. 'Riley, I don't know. I honestly don't know. But there's a foster mother. She'll probably be able to help. You have keys to the house. Everything that a five-year-old boy needs will be there. And it will probably help Finn if you take his own things to help him settle.'

The light in the office was dimmer than the rest of the hospital. But Riley's hurt green eyes were the thing she could see clearest. She was standing right in front of him. Closer than she'd ever wanted to get.

He closed his eyes for a second then nodded. 'You're right. I know you're right. But my son… Finn…he's been in foster care. Isn't that supposed to be terrible?'

She gave a soft smile. 'I think those days are long gone. Foster carers have to go through a mountain of checks these days. Finn will have been well looked after. But the last few days will probably have been a blur.'

He reached out and took her hand in his. It made her catch her breath. It was so unexpected. And more. He just didn't let it go.

She could almost feel his pain. It was palpable. It was right there in the air between them. Riley Callaghan had just had the legs swept from clean under him. And, to his credit, he was still standing. Just the way she would have expected of him.

'Will you help me, April?' He squeezed her hand.

Fear swept through her. 'What do you mean?'

'I don't know. I don't know anything. Will you help me?'

Help. What did that mean? She was all for supporting a colleague in a difficult situation. But this one was probably bigger than anyone could have expected.

'Please? I'm out of my depth, April. I know that already.' His green eyes were pleading with her. Twisting her insides this way and that.

A child. A little boy had just lost a parent. Finn

must be feeling lost. He must feel as if his whole world had just ended.

She met Riley's gaze. 'I'll help where I can,' she said cautiously. 'I can help you with the funeral.'

He frowned. 'You will?'

Mallory. She'd organised every tiny detail of the funeral, even though it had ripped her heart out. Who else knew her twin better than her?

She nodded. 'Let's just say I'm good at funerals.'

And she squeezed his hand back.

CHAPTER TWO

WHAT ON EARTH am I doing?

April spent the whole time on the motorway questioning herself. Riley's hands gripped the steering wheel so tightly his knuckles were white. He'd looked pale this morning. As if he hadn't slept a wink.

By the time the satnav took them into the Birmingham street, the tension was so high she felt as if it could propel the car into the sky. As he killed the engine she leaned over and put one of her hands over his. She really didn't want to touch him. Touching Riley did strange things to her senses, but this wasn't about her. This was about a little boy.

'Stop.'

'What?'

'Just…stop.'

He pulled back his hands and sat back in the seat. 'What are you talking about?'

She could see the tension across his shoulders, reaching up into his jaw.

'You can't go in there like this.'

'What?' The anger that had been simmering beneath the surface was threatening to crack through.

'This is the first time Finn will see you. None of this is his fault. He's about to meet his dad— someone he's only seen in a photograph before.'

She lifted up her hand as Riley opened his mouth to speak. 'I thought about this last night. I told you I don't have any experience with kids, but what do I think this little boy needs to hear?' She leaned a little closer to him. 'I think he needs to hear his dad loves him. His dad is going to look after him and stay with him. His dad is his family and you'll always be together.'

He frowned and then his face relaxed and he shook his head. 'I know. I know that's exactly what I should say.' He lifted one hand and ran it through his hair. 'I spoke to my brother last night.'

Her stomach twisted. 'Isn't he in Scotland?'

Riley nodded. 'He's on a training exercise. There's supposed to be radio silence. But the Colonel made some arrangements for me. Dan was blown away. Says he can't wait to meet Finn.'

'Good. That's great. At least you know you'll have the support of your family.' Then she tilted her head to the side. Something seemed just a little off. 'What aren't you saying? Did you speak to your mum and dad?'

He shook his head and put one hand back on the steering wheel. 'That's the one thing Dan actually understands. My mum and dad will be great. They'll be overwhelmed. They've always wanted a grandchild. But—'

'But what? Don't you need all the help you can get?'

Riley hesitated. 'My mum…has the best of intentions. I love her. I really do. But she'll want to take over. She'll pick up her life and sweep right down.'

'Ah…and you don't want that?'

Riley smiled. 'Maybe…eventually. But right now I need to get to know Finn. I need to spend some time with him. Like I said, I have no idea about five-year-old boys.'

April shook her head. 'Well, that's a strange thing to say.'

He shrugged. 'Why?'

She lifted her hands. 'Because you've been one. Your brother has been one. You know all you need to know about five-year-old boys.'

He shifted in his seat and pulled his phone from his pocket. 'Look at this.' He opened an app. 'This is what I bought last night.'

She leaned forward to glance at the screen and couldn't help the little laugh that came out. 'A parenting guide? You bought a parenting guide?' She started shaking her head.

'What? I told you. I don't know anything. Anything at all.'

She leaned back against the seat and looked over at him. Riley Callaghan was just about to change before her eyes. The doctor, the soldier and the cheeky charmer was about to take on a whole new role. She admired him for his fear. She admired him for wanting to get to know Finn without letting his mother take over.

Her mouth dried. This was a whole world that she'd never know. She'd already made the decision. She'd never have kids. Her biological clock would never be allowed to tick. When her sister had died it had almost been like watching herself in a mirror. Mallory hadn't had the information that she had. April's genetic testing had only been approved because of Mallory's diagnosis and a look back through the family history. If she ignored the results she would be disrespecting her sister's memory. She could never do that.

But this time of year was especially hard. Her heart gave a little squeeze as she thought of her parents. Before this—before any of this—her mother had always joked she would like a house filled with grandchildren once she retired. But that would never happen now.

And even though her mum and dad fully supported her decision, she knew they had a secret ache for the future life they were losing.

'April?'

Riley's voice pulled her from her thoughts. She gave him a soft smile and wrestled in her pocket for her own phone. She turned it around so he could see her Internet search: *Top ten Christmas toys for five-year-old boys.*

Riley groaned. 'Christmas. It's only six weeks away. I made no plans because I thought I'd be in Sierra Leone. I don't even have a Christmas tree.'

'It's the middle of November. You have time.'

He was staring at her with those bright green eyes. There was silence for a few seconds. She shifted in her seat and brought her hand up to wipe her cheek. 'What is it—do I have something on my face?'

'Why wouldn't you talk to me before?'

She was surprised. 'I did. We spoke about patients all the time.'

He gave a gentle shake of his head. 'But you wouldn't talk to me about anything else.' He paused and continued with his curious stare. 'April, why did you tell me you were good at funerals?'

She could sense his wariness in asking the question. But he'd still asked. He was like this at work too. He always asked patients the difficult questions. Always spoke to the surgeons about the risks and possibilities.

This time he reached out and touched her hand. 'April, did you lose someone? Were you married?'

She closed her eyes for a second. Riley had only been there four weeks. Word obviously hadn't reached him. Then again, the turnover of staff at Waterloo Court could be high. Not everyone knew her background and she preferred it that way.

This wasn't normally something she would share. But she'd just shared a major part of Riley's life. If they'd been on the ward, she would have found a way to dodge the question. But, alone in the confines of the car, there was nowhere to hide. And she didn't want to tell a lie.

'I lost my sister,' she said quietly.

The warmth of his hand was flooding through her system. 'When?'

'Eighteen months ago.'

'Was it an accident?'

She licked her lips. She should have known he would press for more details. This was hard. Probably because she hadn't really shared with anyone before. Probably because she didn't want them to figure out the next step. 'No. It wasn't an accident.' The rest of the words stuck somewhere in the back of her throat. She didn't mention the cancer. She didn't mention the fact they were twins. She didn't mention the genetic tests. These were all things that Riley Callaghan didn't need to know.

By some grace, he didn't ask any more. He didn't ask those details. 'You organised the funeral?'

She nodded. 'She was my sister. My mum and dad were devastated—we all were—but it seemed the one thing I could do that made me feel a little better, a little more in control.' She took a deep breath and met his gaze, trying not to think that his hand was still covering hers. 'So, I can help you with that. If I can find a few of Isabel's friends, talk to some of them, I can make the practical arrangements for you, and you can focus on Finn.'

At the mention of Finn's name again she sensed him tense. 'Riley,' she said warningly.

'What?'

'You're tensing. You're angry. You've been angry the whole drive up here. That's no use. No use at all.' She was talking to him firmly, the way she usually spoke to a patient who was just about ready to give up on their physio.

He snapped. 'What do you expect? I've been cheated out of five years of my son's life. If I'd known about Finn, I would have been there. If Isabel had been involved in an accident, at least my little boy would know he would be with someone who loved and cared about him. He doesn't know any of that. I'm a stranger to him. She did that.'

She shook her head at him. 'Don't you dare.'

'Don't dare what?' He was almost indignant.

She pulled her hand out from under his and pointed her finger at him. 'Don't you dare go in there simmering with resentment at Finn's mother. You're an adult. Deal with it. Deal with the fact that life doesn't always give you the hand of cards that you want. Finn will need you to talk about his mum. If he hears resentment or anger in your voice he'll close off to you. You'll wreck your relationship before it even has a chance to form.'

'I thought you didn't know anything about kids?'

'I don't. But I know enough about people. And so do you. You're a doctor. You deal with families all the time.' She dropped her hand and let her voice soften. 'I know you're angry. And if you are, talk to me. Talk to your brother.' She stared out of the window at the blue sky above them. 'My sister and I used to do a thing.'

'A thing?'

She nodded. 'If either of us was angry or

upset—and it happened a lot—we used to hug it out.'

'You what?'

She shrugged. 'Hugging. Physical contact. Scientifically proven to reduce stress and anxiety. To release tension.'

He looked amused. 'You want me to hug it out?'

The expression on his face was incredulous. She unclipped her seat belt and opened her arms. 'Why not? You can't go in there all tense and angry. That doesn't help you. That doesn't help Finn.' She raised her eyebrows. 'And, just so you know, this is a one-time offer.'

His face broke into a smile as he shook his head and unclipped his own belt. 'I must be crazy.'

'I've heard you called worse.'

He leaned forward and wrapped his arms around her. Riley Callaghan knew how to hug. This was no gentle, delicate hug. This was a massive pick-you-up-and-swing-you-round bear hug. Just as well they were in the car.

His emerging stubble brushed against her cheek. The waft of soap and masculinity flooded through her senses. That whole sensation of being held by a man, being comforted by someone who wrapped you in their arms, made her catch her breath. It had been so long. So long since she'd let someone this close.

She was doing this for him. Not for her.

So why did it feel like this?

He couldn't see her face, so she closed her eyes for a few seconds. Letting herself just remember the moment. Feel the heat, the warmth and the comfort.

She'd missed this. Missed this contact more than she'd ever expected to. What she'd done with the best of intentions had turned into something that was kind of overwhelming.

His voice murmured in her ear. 'Thanks, April.'

'No problem,' she replied automatically. Lost in the warm breath near her ear.

After the longest time he pulled back.

'Okay,' he said. 'We're all hugged out.' She could see how nervous he was. 'It's time for me to meet my son.'

In the blink of an eye his life had changed.

He was a father. His first priority was his son.

April was a godsend.

His first sight of Finn, sitting on the edge of his

bed in the foster home, ripped his heart clean out of his chest. Finn was his living image. If he'd sat his five-year-old self down next to Finn they would have looked like twins.

He'd never need a DNA test.

He'd wondered about the photo last night—if it was really a good representation of Finn. If they really looked that alike. Now he knew.

The foster carer was possibly the greatest human being he'd ever met. All preconceived ideas were swept out the window in a matter of seconds. She was used to taking kids in crisis situations and was very experienced. She even ran rings around the po-faced Ms Cummings.

She was warm and friendly. She knew Riley and Finn hadn't met before and had already made a little list of things Finn had mentioned in the last few days. That included things from home he wanted, a list of clothing he would need, the contact details of his school and a few names of friends of his mum's.

April stayed in the background, just accepting the lists with a gracious nod and leaving Riley to ask all the questions that he wanted.

It hadn't taken much to notice the slight tremor

in Finn's hands. Riley had sat down on the bed next to him and spoke to his son for the first time. He'd never been so terrified in his life. Not when he'd been serving, not when he'd been retrieving military casualties and not when he'd been stranded on a battlefield with virtually no equipment. This was a whole new ball game.

Somehow it felt good that April was there to have his back. She didn't interfere. She just stayed in the background. That hug in the car had done weird things to his mind. Her body pressed against his had sent a quick flash of a few thoughts he'd had about her in the past four weeks. The vanilla scent that had drifted up his nose had taken him to a whole other place. One where April wasn't permanently dressed in her physiotherapist uniform.

Today was the first day he'd seen her in something else. She was wearing a dress. A dress. He hadn't thought of April as a dress sort of girl. It was dark, covered with assorted pink butterflies, finishing just above her knees, which were covered in thick dark tights and knee-high black boots. She'd wrapped a pink scarf around her neck and was wearing a black military-style jacket.

She even looked as if she had a little make-up on. Either that or her lashes were darker than normal and highlighting those blue eyes. He'd never seen April outside the work environment and somehow it felt as if he'd been missing out.

April Henderson looked good. But then he'd always thought that.

And she'd been right. He'd needed to leave his resentment at the door. One look at Finn told him that.

Finn was charming. Polite, well mannered, and the first thing he told him was that he was going to be an astronaut. Riley smiled. He remembered having the same ambition. His little voice shook when he spoke about his mum and Riley wrapped his arm around his shoulder and pulled him close. 'I'm sorry, Finn. I'm sorry about the accident. But I'll look after you now. I'm your dad. I didn't know about you before, but I know about you now.'

He'd pulled Finn up onto his lap. 'If you want to, we'll go and get some of your things. You can bring whatever you want.'

'I can go back home?'

It was like staring into his own green eyes, but these little eyes were laced with uncertainty. Riley tried to keep his voice steady. 'You're going to stay with me now. But your mum's house will stay as it is for now. We can collect your clothes, your toys, some photographs and anything else you want.' He ran his hand over his son's brown hair. Finn had the same little kink in his hair that he did. 'I know some people who will be so happy to meet you. Your uncle Dan has just flown out to Afghanistan. But he's already sent me a message for you. And your gran and grand-dad will be really happy to meet you too.'

Riley's mouth was running away with him. He could see the tiny tremble in Finn's hands. It made his heart ache. Should he squeeze him harder? He wasn't quite sure.

'I have a gran and granddad?' Finn's eyes widened. 'I never had those before.'

Yes, you did. You just didn't know it.

He resisted the temptation to say the words out loud. 'Well, you do now.'

It wasn't just Finn's hands that were trembling; it was his voice too. Riley had spent his life as a doctor seeing things that affected him deep down. He'd wished a million times he could change things for the patients he worked with. But he'd never wished he could change things more than he did right now. He'd do anything to take away the hurt in Finn's eyes.

Finn looked up shyly across the room, as if he were searching for something. Riley had the oddest sensation.

'Who is the lady?'

Riley shifted on the bed. 'The lady?'

'The pretty one with the blonde hair. Is she your girlfriend?' There was an almost hopeful edge to Finn's voice.

Riley followed Finn's gaze. April was talking quietly with the foster mum, scribbling down a few more notes. He wasn't quite sure what to say.

Something washed over him as he watched the expression on Finn's face. He was right on Riley's knee but it was almost as if he were trying to anchor himself. Finn had spent his whole life brought up by his mum and, from the sound of it, mainly in the company of her friends. His heart squeezed. That was why he was looking at April.

He was used to being with women. Being in

the company of a male from this point onwards would be a huge deal for Finn. Riley squeezed his eyes closed for the briefest of seconds as he remembered all the things his mum used to do with him and his brother as kids. Climbing into bed for cuddles, secret cake baking, her patience with homework, and the way one look could let him know that everything would be all right. It was only in the last few years he'd realised that even though she could be overpowering, how central she'd been for him and his brother. Finn had lost that. He'd lost his central point. Could Riley ever hope to become that person for Finn? Or would he always look for a mother figure in his life?

Riley's skin was pale. 'That's April. She's my... friend.' Was she? 'She works with me at the hospital. She's a physiotherapist. She helps people get well again. Sometimes she has to help them walk again.' It seemed the simplest explanation.

Finn frowned. 'If Uncle Dan is in Afghanistan, will you have to go there too?' His voice had a little tremble. 'What will happen to me?'

And, just like that, the thoughts from last night filled his brain again.

He loved his job. He loved the postings. They fired his enthusiasm and ignited his passion. The last four weeks had been fine, but only because he'd known it wouldn't be for long.

His heart twisted in his chest as he said the words he had to out loud. 'It's you and me, Finn. I won't be going away again. I'll be staying here, with you.'

He looked up. April had appeared in the doorway. He could see the expression on her face. She'd heard him in the last few weeks. Being excited about his future plans, talking about all the missions he'd been on.

The Colonel had phoned him this morning. He could stay at Waterloo Court for the next six months. He had temporary family accommodation. This was his life now. Part of him ached. But he pushed it away. He gave April an almost imperceptible nod.

He'd decided. His son would come first. Always.

She could tell he was struggling. And she felt like an intruder, watching two people who were alike in so many ways getting to know each other for the first time.

The visit to the house was the hardest. And she could relate to this. She really could. She'd had to pack up her sister's house and give away some of her belongings. She'd heard other people talk about it in the past, but you could never really appreciate how hard something like this was until you had to do it yourself.

She fingered her necklace as they reached the house. Two intertwined gold hearts. Her parents had given Mallory and April the same thing for their twenty-first birthdays. Mallory had been buried wearing hers.

The first surprise when they reached the house was the tree.

It seemed that Isabel loved Christmas and even though it was only November the tree was already up and covered in decorations.

'We did that last week,' Finn said shakily.

April knelt down and looked at some of the decorations on the tree. She could see instantly they'd been made by a child's hands.

'Will we take some of these too? You made these, didn't you?'

Finn nodded and pointed to a few of them, which April folded into some tissue paper that she found.

She'd done the practical things. She'd found all the clothes and packed them up. She'd helped Finn choose all the toys and books he'd wanted. Then she'd taken a deep breath and thought about all the sentimental things the foster carer had spoken to her about.

'Photos,' she whispered to Riley. 'We need to find some photos for Finn to have of his mum.'

Riley knelt down in front of Finn. 'Should we get some photographs? Pictures of you and Mum we can put in your new bedroom?'

Finn gave a nod and broke into a run. 'This one,' he shouted. 'This is the one I have.'

April glanced at it and her heart gave a little flip. It was a picture of Isabel and Riley together. They were in a pub somewhere. He had his arm around her shoulders and they were looking at each other and laughing. It looked as if it could have been taken yesterday.

It was like a little spear hitting inside her.

Why? She instantly pushed the feeling aside. She'd no right to feel like that. Riley and her weren't anything to each other. Never could be. She wasn't at that point in her life. And he had his hands more than full for the next while.

Riley's face had blanched. The letter had said Finn had a photograph of his dad; he must not have expected Isabel to be in it too.

April bent down and took the photo frame. 'This is a good photo, Finn. I like it a lot. But let's take some other photographs too. Ones of you and your mum together.'

Finn nodded and darted through to the main living room. April followed his lead and took a photograph from the wall he pointed at, and a calendar from the kitchen that had different photographs of them for every month of the year.

'And the stick!' said Finn. He jumped on top of a chair and found something on a shelf. 'My mum has all our pictures on this!'

Riley gave a nod and put the USB stick in his pocket.

He bent back down. 'Finn, do you want to take anything else?'

Finn hesitated. There was clearly something in his mind.

A wave of something came over April. She'd

packed up Finn's bedding to take with him. But after her sister had died, when she'd been packing up the house, she'd collapsed onto the bed at some point and been overwhelmed by the familiar scent from her sister's pillow. She'd sobbed for hours.

She brushed her hand against Riley's. 'I think I know,' she whispered.

She reached out with her other hand and touched Finn's head. 'Should we take some other things of your mum's? How about her pillow, or a blanket that she used? Is there a jumper she loved? Do you want to take something like that?'

Riley squeezed her hand. He must know what this was doing to her. But his look was pure gratitude.

Finn sniffed. So April took his hand and gathered up the things he showed her. He buried his face in his mother's pillow for a few seconds and let out a sob. She couldn't help herself. She gathered the little boy into her arms and just held him. 'I know, honey. I know how hard this is. I'm right here with you. And so is your dad.'

The little body crumpled against hers and a tear slid down her cheek.

This wasn't about her. This wasn't about the family of her own that she'd never have. This was about a little boy who was desperately sad. But somehow it felt about both.

Riley seemed choked too. They gathered up the rest of the belongings and he walked Finn out to the car.

'Wait,' she said. Something had just struck her. She pulled out her phone. 'Let's get a picture of the two of you together.'

Finn looked up at his dad. 'Can we?'

Riley seemed surprised at the question. He knelt down and wrapped his arm around Finn's shoulder. 'Absolutely. I'd love a picture of us both together.'

She knew she should capture it. A first picture of father and son together. But the smile Riley plastered on his face didn't quite reach his eyes. They were still full of worry. As for Finn? He just looked a little nervous. As if he didn't quite know what would come next.

She snapped a few. 'Perfect,' she said.

Riley strapped Finn into the car. As she walked around to her side of the car, he pulled her hand and stopped her, spinning her around to face him.

'April, I just wanted to say something.'

Her heartbeat quickened. It was starting to get dark. Collecting the things had taken a little longer than expected. It had been such a big day. One she'd never expected to be part of.

Today was a Saturday. She might have gone into work for a few hours—even though she wasn't on duty. She'd planned on working with Jake today, but when she'd phoned and left a message for him he'd been absolutely fine. The only other thing she would have done was pick up a few things for dinner.

As it was cold she might even have stayed in her pyjamas all day and watched Christmas movies on TV. Part of her knew that if life had gone as planned, she would probably have had a little pang about not going to Riley's drinks last night. She would have had a twinge of regret that she wouldn't see him again. But part of that would have been reassuring.

It would have left her clear to lock away the attraction she'd been trying to ignore for the last four weeks. She could have parcelled it up in a box like a Christmas present and stored it away in a cupboard. That would have been so much simpler than any of this.

Before she had time to think, Riley slid his hand behind her waist and pulled her towards him, resting his forehead against hers.

It was so up close and personal. They were at the back of the car. Finn couldn't see them. The temperature had dropped; their warm breath was visible in the cold air.

A wave of emotions swept through her. She'd seen a whole other side of Riley Callaghan today. There had already been a glimmer of attraction. Now, she'd seen him at his most exposed. She'd been there when he'd got the news about Finn, then met his child for the first time. It felt too big. Too much. More than she could handle right now.

Finn was adorable. He pulled at every heart-string she had. In a way she knew that she'd picked up some things that Riley might have missed. Riley would be a good father; he just had to get to know his little boy first.

Her heart flipped over. That parent relation-ship. The one she'd never have. The one she'd never even allowed herself to think about since she'd made her decision. For a few seconds today she'd felt…something. Even if it was only tiny. That urge to reach out to help a child in need. She pressed her lips together and tried to push all the emotions away.

She had to think about the surgery. She had to think about preparing herself. She didn't need her heart tangled up in this mess. She had to keep it somewhere safe.

She hadn't moved. His head was still pressed against hers.

'Thank you,' he whispered. 'Thank you for coming here with me today.'

She gulped and pulled back.

'You're a colleague. No problem.' Her hand brushed against a piece of paper she'd pushed into her pocket. 'I think it's best if you and Finn have some time to yourselves now. I've got a couple of numbers of friends from Isabel's phone book. I'll talk to them to get an idea of what she would have liked. They might want to help with the arrangements.'

A frown furrowed Riley's brow. 'That would be great, thank you.' The words were pleasant but the look on his face told her something different. It was almost as if she'd just abandoned him on a cross-country hike with no provisions.

And he didn't say another word until he dropped her back at her house.

CHAPTER THREE

THE THING ABOUT life throwing you a curveball meant that you didn't always get things right. Finn was the easiest and best part of it all. Riley had heard children were resilient and Finn was still hesitant around him.

But they'd set up his room the way he wanted, hung up his clothes and established a little routine. When he'd heard Finn crying in bed one night, he'd just gone in, wrapped his arms around him and lay with him until he stopped.

He now knew that Finn hated peas, liked chicken in all forms, was also partial to sausages and tomato ketchup, and loved a kids' TV show with spacemen. He had seven DVDs of it and Riley had watched them all with him.

The whirlwind that was Riley's mother was a whole other matter. Thank goodness he hadn't seen her in the flesh when he'd told her about Finn. He was pretty sure she'd had a heart attack at the other end of the phone. Of course she was driving right down. She wanted to meet her grandchild straight away. She'd asked a million questions that Riley didn't know the answers to.

Eventually he'd told her a white lie. He told her that the social worker had recommended that he and Finn spend the first week together on their own to get used to each other. Not to overwhelm him with things. In fact, the social worker had recommended routine as soon as possible. So he'd registered Finn at school and taken him in to say hello. The headmistress had been great, suggesting he bring Finn in for a few hours in the first instance to let him find his feet.

Riley had finally managed to placate his mother by sending the picture that April had taken of them both together. She'd cried at that point. But at least it had given him some time.

What he couldn't work out right now was how to be around April.

Since they'd picked up Finn together, she'd retreated right into herself again. She'd spoken to him about a few funeral arrangements she'd helped put together after talking to Isabel's friends. She'd asked him to speak to Finn about a few things too. But that was it.

No closeness. No real glimmer of friendship.

Maybe it was his fault? If she'd planned her sister's funeral, had she had to deal with other things too? Maybe empty her house, or deal with all her financial affairs. She'd seemed so knowledgeable in Isabel's house—a place he'd felt entirely uncomfortable. She'd seemed to know exactly what Finn needed—even though she said she had no more experience of children than he had. The visit might have revived memories for her that he hadn't considered. Was it any wonder she was keeping her distance?

The rest of the staff had been great. They'd been surprised he was still there. But the news had spread quickly, and everyone was supportive.

Finn had asked to stay at school today until lunchtime. That meant he had three hours. Hours best spent in the hospital.

He'd barely got across the doorway before someone gave him a shout. April.

'Dr Callaghan? Can you come and assess Robert Black for me, please?' He could see the concern on her face straight away.

He nodded and walked over quickly. Robert had been caught in an explosion. His spinal injury was severe and he was currently in neurogenic shock. This was always a crucial time for patients. Neurogenic shock happened in almost half of patients with a spinal injury above T6 in the first twenty-four hours and didn't go away for between one to three weeks. Patients in neurogenic shock needed continual assessment of their circulation, senses and breathing abilities. Neurogenic shock could lead to organ failure.

Robert Black's blood pressure was low, his heart rate bradycardic. His limbs were flaccid, his skin warm and flushed due to the vasodilation caused by the neurogenic shock.

Riley signalled to the nurse. 'Connie, can you get me some atropine?'

She nodded and handed him a vial from the emergency trolley. April moved automatically to the head of the bed to keep assessing Robert's breathing. The staff here were used to emergencies and good at recognising the symptoms.

Riley kept his voice calm and even as he flushed the atropine through the Venflon in Robert's arm. 'Robert, I'm just giving you something to speed up your heart rate a little. I'm also going to give you something to help your blood pressure.'

He nodded at Connie again. 'Get me some dopamine.' He turned to April. 'Can you put some oxygen on for me, please?'

April nodded and slipped the mask over Robert's face, lowering her head to the bed to monitor the rise and fall of his chest and keeping her eyes on the numbers on the oximeter.

Teamwork was crucial. Neurogenic shock was difficult. It was different from spinal shock or the most common type of shock with injuries—hypovolemic—and had to be treated differently. Often patients could have a respiratory arrest.

Right on cue, April waved her hand. 'Can we call an anaesthetist?'

'No time,' said Riley as he finished administering the dopamine and moved to the head of the bed. It only took a few seconds to tilt Robert's head back, using the laryngoscope to insert an endotracheal tube.

He glanced towards the doorway. 'We need to transfer him to high dependency. Does anyone know if they have a bed?'

April took his cue and ran over to the phone.

Riley kept bagging the patient. At this stage, Robert needed to be ventilated. He could only pray this was a temporary setback.

Robert's regular doctor appeared at the door. His eyes widened. 'What the—?'

He stopped himself and held open the ward doors. 'High dependency?'

April put the phone down and nodded. 'They'll be waiting.'

He moved over and grabbed a side of the bed. Between the other doctor, April and the nurse, the transfer was smooth. Riley concentrated on the airway, bagging the whole way, then setting up the ventilators and pressures when they arrived.

'Need anything else?' he asked his colleague.

The doctor shook his head. 'I take it he had just had a rapid deterioration?'

Riley nodded. 'April was working with him. She picked up on it straight away.'

'Thank goodness. This could have been a disaster.'

Riley gave a thoughtful nod and stared back towards the door. April had stopped in the corridor. He gave a brief smile. 'Give me a page if you need any help.'

The other doctor nodded and he headed out into the corridor.

April was dressed in her usual attire of the physios, white tunic and navy trousers, with her hair pulled back in a ponytail. She had her eyes closed and was resting her head and body against the wall.

He touched her arm and her eyes jerked open. 'April, are you okay?'

Their eyes connected for a few moments. Hers were bluer than ever. Maybe it was the bright hospital lights. Or maybe it was the fact he was noticing so much more about her. April had always looked away quickly before, but this time she didn't. This time it felt as if there was more to their gaze.

But she pulled her arm away. 'Of course, I'm fine.' She gave her head a little shake. 'I just got a fright when Robert deteriorated so quickly.'

He nodded. As a doctor, he was used to dealing with emergencies, but other staff didn't have the same exposure as he did. Quite often they did a debrief after things like this.

'Come with me.'

Her eyes widened. 'What?' She shook her head fiercely. 'No, I've got work to do. I need to get back to the ward.'

'Actually, you don't.'

She glared at him and folded her arms across her chest. 'I can't.'

He spoke firmly. 'You can. Get your jacket. I have to pick up Finn at twelve. But we have time for a coffee before I go get him.'

April shifted on her feet. 'I have work to do.'

'You must be due a break, and we need a chance to debrief—to talk about what just happened. We usually do it as a team after any emergency. Let's take some time out.'

She hesitated and took a few breaths. He gestured towards the locker room. 'Go and get your jacket.' He wasn't going to let this go. There was something in that glance. Some kind of connection.

She gave the briefest nod then disappeared for a few seconds while his stomach gave a little roll.

No getting away from it. April Henderson had definitely been avoiding him. He just had to figure out why.

* * *

Her hands were still shaking as she opened her locker and grabbed her jacket. The canteen and coffee shop were across the main courtyard. She slid her hands into her puffy winter jacket. Riley was waiting for her at the door.

This was nothing. It was a simple chat. A debrief. She had heard of them before—she'd just never needed one.

So why was her stomach flip flopping around?

She'd spent the last few days avoiding Riley. She'd done the things she'd been asked to do. The funeral arrangements were sorted. She'd arranged the undertaker, the church, the minister and the plot at the cemetery. According to Isabel's friends, she'd been a little unconventional. One had offered to speak. Another had offered to say a poem. She just had to find out what Riley would think appropriate for Finn. She figured he'd want to give Finn the chance to say goodbye to his mum. She just wasn't quite sure how a kid did that.

She lifted her bag. All the paperwork and arrangements were inside. She just had to hand them over.

Riley was holding the door open. Large flakes of snow were falling outside. Even though it was still morning, the sky had a grey tinge.

They started walking across the courtyard. 'Coffee shop or canteen?'

April shrugged. 'Either.'

'How hungry are you? Do you want an early lunch?'

She shook her head.

'Then coffee shop it is.'

They walked over to the coffee shop and he held the door for her again. 'Take a seat. I'll get the coffee.'

She sat down on a red fabric sofa next to the lit fire. There was a garland above the fireplace and red tinsel adorning the walls. November. Another place with decorations. The music being piped around the room was a medley of Christmas songs. She smiled. This would have driven Mallory crazy. She used to say that Christmas seemed to begin as soon as Halloween had finished.

A few minutes later Riley appeared, carrying a tray. She looked up as she shrugged her way out of her jacket. The heat from the fire was already reaching her.

He smiled as he set down the two tall latte glasses filled with hot chocolate, with whipped cream and marshmallows spilling over the edges. A plate with shortbread Christmas trees followed.

She looked up. 'Really?'

His eyes twinkled. 'Why not? I love Christmas.'

There was something about that smile. Something about that twinkle in his eye. It had always been there before, and it was part of the reason she'd avoided him. Riley Callaghan was too easy to like. He was almost infectious.

She was surprised. 'You do? So do I.'

'At last.' He smiled. 'Something we have in common.'

She frowned. 'I imagined you were always away for Christmas.'

He looked amused. 'You think about me?' He couldn't hide the cheeky gleam in his eyes. Then he shrugged. 'A lot of the time I am. But here's the thing…' He leaned across the table as if he were going to whisper to her.

She followed his lead and bowed her head next to his as his face lit up with a wicked grin. 'Many other places in the world do Christmas too. Sometimes in forty degrees. And if they don't? Well, I can always take it with me.'

She sat back and shook her head, pointing her finger on the table. 'Well, I don't want a sunny Christmas or to be anywhere else. I like Christmas *here*. I like tacky Christmas songs. I *really* like it when it snows. I like Advent calendars, Christmas cards and—' she winked at him '—I really like Christmas food.'

She spooned some of the cream into her mouth.

'So do I,' he said cheekily as he dug his spoon into her cream instead of his.

'Hey!'

She gave his hand a playful slap. 'Watch out, Riley. I bite, you know.'

His gaze met hers for a few seconds. He didn't speak. Just kept staring at her. As if he were contemplating a whole host of things to say. A whole type of discussion she just couldn't think about right now.

She broke their gaze and dug her spoon back into the cream.

'About today,' he started. She looked up. Work. This felt like safe territory.

'You did everything right. There is always a

risk of sudden deterioration in patients with neurogenic shock. It can happen at any point. You picked it up well.'

She sighed and leaned her head on her hand. The teasing and fun had finished, but that was fine. This was what they really should be talking about. 'But he's ventilated now. That can't be good.'

Riley nodded. 'It's not great. It is a deterioration. Now, we need to monitor carefully in case he's going into organ failure. He might not.'

She met his gaze. She felt sad. His emerald-green eyes were saying a whole lot of things that they weren't discussing out loud. They both knew that things for Robert might not be good.

He leaned across and touched her hand. 'You did everything you should.'

She stared down at his blunt cut fingernails. She should pull her hand back. Jerk it away. She wanted to. But somehow after the events earlier she wanted a few seconds of comfort.

She looked up again. 'How is Finn?' It was the question she should have asked immediately. It didn't matter she was trying to step back and detach herself from the situation. She'd spent the last few days worrying about the little guy.

Riley took a long slow breath. 'He's not happy, but he's not sad. He's getting there. He's met some school friends and the teacher says he's fitting in well. They're going to do some bereavement work at school with him because it's still all so new.' He stirred his hot chocolate. 'He was crying in bed the other night.'

Her heart squeezed in her chest. 'What did you do?'

He pressed his lips together. 'I thought about it for about ten seconds. Then I climbed in next to him and just held him. What else could I do? I hate that he's sad. I hate that this has happened to him. I know the upheaval must be awful. And my learning curve is steep.'

'What have you done?'

A smile crept onto his lips. 'Well, my fridge and freezer are now stocked with child-friendly foods. I never knew there were so many yogurts. Potatoes have to be mashed. Raisins have to be a particular brand and he'll only eat Pink Lady apples.'

April smiled as she spooned marshmallows

into her hot chocolate. 'But that all sounds good. It sounds as though he's settling.'

Riley nodded. 'We've put up the pictures you brought from the house. It's weird. Seeing Isabel all around me.'

He dropped his head and stopped speaking.

Something inside her lurched. A horrible feeling. Envy. Why on earth was she feeling that? It was so misplaced. So wrong. But it was definitely there. Maybe there had been more to the relationship than she'd initially thought. 'So...do you miss her?'

He sighed; the pained expression on his face said it all. 'That's just it, April. I didn't really know her that well. We only went out for a couple of months. I don't have a million nice tales I can tell Finn about his mum. I don't have a lot of memories. She was nice.' He shrugged his shoulders. 'How awful is that? That's about as much as I have to say about her. Finn deserves more than that.'

She licked her lips for a second. She could see what he wasn't saying. 'You're still angry.'

He pulled a face. 'Inside, I am. But I hope I don't show that around Finn. It's just when I turn

around Isabel seems to be staring me in the face.'
He ran his fingers through his hair. 'And the family housing. It's not ideal. You probably already know that. I need to find a place for us. A home.'

The way he said those words sent a little pang through her. Riley wanted to make a home with his son. Would she ever get to make a home with someone? Would anyone want to be in a relationship with a girl who could always have a cancer risk hanging over her head, and couldn't have a family? It wouldn't exactly make for a winning profile on a dating website. She cringed at the thought of it and focused back on Riley.

'You can't just jump out and buy the first thing you see.'

'Can't I? Why not? I can get a mortgage. I have enough money in the bank.'

'But you don't know if you'll always be here. Another move might not be good for Finn.'

'But what if it's a permanent move?'

Riley Callaghan. Here permanently. Working together every day. She'd need to see his smiling face. Avoid his cheeky grins. Four weeks had been manageable—there had been an end date in sight. But for ever? How could she lock away the attraction she felt for him for ever?

She leaned back in her chair. 'It's a lot to think about.' She glanced at the glass in front of her. 'This must be a million calories. You—' she wagged her finger at him '—are a bad influence.'

He leaned forward. 'Just call it a bribe.'

He had that grin on his face again. The one he used time and time again on the ward when he wanted to talk someone into something.

She pointed at the shortbread Christmas trees. 'Am I going to need one of these?'

He pushed the whole plate before her and clasped his hands on the table. It seemed such a formal stance for Riley she almost laughed.

'Thing is,' he started seriously, 'I appreciate all the arrangements you've made for me. I know doing something like that really goes above and beyond.' He pointed at the hot chocolate and shortbread. 'And these don't count for that.' He waved his hand. 'I'll get you something more appropriate.' He leaned a little closer across the table. 'But there's something else.'

She shook her head and ignored the 'more appropriate' comment. Riley Callaghan was trying to sweet-talk her. 'Don't build it up, Riley. Just hit me with it.'

He did. 'Finn.'

She narrowed her gaze. 'What about Finn?'

He sighed. 'I haven't had that conversation yet—the one about the funeral. And I was hoping you might help me do it.'

She sat back again. But Riley kept going. 'I'm still taking baby steps here. I don't want to do anything wrong. And I could ask my mother, but then—' he shook his head '—that would just open the floodgates for her to bulldoze all over us.'

'Has your mother met Finn yet?'

He shook his head. 'I'm holding her at bay. I've told her the social worker advised to give him a few days to settle.'

She opened her mouth. 'You what?'

He held up his hand. 'You haven't met my mother—yet. Don't judge.'

She folded her arms across her chest. 'What exactly is it you want me to do, Riley? I'm not sure I should be getting involved. This is really something you and Finn should work through together.'

'I'm scared.'

He said the words right out of the blue.

And she couldn't catch her breath.

'What if I make a mess of this, April? Do I say Finn's too young to be at a funeral and everything should go on without him, or do I insist he attends when he really isn't ready for it? Do I ask him what he wants to do? At five, how can he even know?'

Anguish and pain were written all over his face. She understood. What had happened on the ward today had just helped open the door for him. He wasn't grieving for Isabel. He was grieving for his son.

'I get that you're scared, Riley. But this is your son. I think you need to have this conversation with him.'

He didn't look any better. He turned a shortbread tree over and over in his hands before finally looking up through dark lashes and meeting her gaze. 'He's been asking for you.'

'What?'

'Finn. He's asked where you were. I think because we brought him back together he's expected to see you again.'

She gulped. The kid was five. He was confused. It wasn't such a strange thought to have. 'I don't want to give him any mixed messages.'

'What mixed messages? Aren't we friends, April?'

She didn't speak. Her brain was flooded with memories of her hands against his chest, his forehead next to hers. All things she didn't need to remember. But they were annoying; they seemed to have seared their way into her brain and cemented themselves there.

She locked gazes with Riley. He'd asked if they were friends.

No. They weren't. Being around Riley was making her feel things she didn't want to. Didn't need to. Life was hard right now. She was clear about her decision. She knew what her next steps would be. Getting involved with anyone would confuse things. They might want to talk. They might have an opinion. Somehow, already, she knew Riley would have an opinion. And she wasn't ready for any of that. After Christmas her ovaries and fallopian tubes would be removed. It wasn't a complete and utter guarantee that she would remain cancer-free, but when the odds were against her it was as good as it could be.

The image of Finn's face clouded her thoughts. He was so like Riley.

It still made her ache. She was trying to stay so strong. But being around a kid as adorable as Finn had made all those children she would never have suddenly feel so real. All those grandkids her mum and dad would never have to entertain. She couldn't help but pine for the life that would never be hers. She stared down at the shortbread Christmas tree. And Christmas made it seem just that little bit harder—because Christmas should be all about family.

She sucked in a breath. How dare she feel sorry for herself right now? The person she should be thinking about was Finn.

She met Riley's gaze. Somehow he knew just when to keep quiet.

She took a deep breath. 'I'll come over tomorrow. I still haven't arranged the flowers. I'll ask Finn if he knows what his mum's favourites were. Maybe if he can help pick something it will help that conversation get started.' She pointed to the pile of paperwork. 'The minister at the church is pretty modern. I told him I'd get back to him about music. If there is a particular song that Finn likes, maybe that's the one to use? I asked Isabel's friends. But they all had different ideas.'

Riley nodded. 'Thank you. I mean that.'

She gave him a smile. 'It's okay.'

'Is it? Until a few days ago we'd never really had a proper conversation. You always seemed to avoid me. When I saw you come into the pub the other night I thought…' His voice tailed off.

'You thought what?'

He shrugged. 'I thought you might actually have come in to have a farewell drink. I thought you might have found it in your heart to be nice to me for five minutes.'

He was teasing her. She knew that. But his words seemed to strike a bit of a nerve. She had the feeling some of it might come from a little deeper.

And there was that little twisting feeling again. He might as well sell corkscrews from the way his words, his looks and his touch affected her.

'I like to keep focused at work. These patients, they've been through enough. They need our full attention. They deserve it.'

He shook his head. 'Oh, no. Don't give me that. You engage perfectly with all the patients. It's only me that gets the cold shoulder; don't think I didn't notice.'

There was a surge of heat into her cheeks. 'Maybe you're just hard to be around, Riley?'

She knew it was a deflection, and as he folded his arms and narrowed his gaze she also knew he wasn't about to let her off.

'So what is it? Why no chat? Why no friendly banter? You seem to do it enough with the patients.'

'Maybe I just don't like to mix work with pleasure.'

As soon as the words left her mouth she realised her mistake.

His eyes gleamed. 'Oh, so I could be pleasure, could I?'

She shook her head and waved her hand. 'Don't be ridiculous. Anyway, you servicemen, you come and go so often. You were only supposed to be covering for four weeks. It's exhausting having to befriend new staff all the time. Sometimes I just don't have the energy.'

His grin had spread from one ear to the other.

It was clear he wasn't listening any more. 'So I'm exhausting, am I? I kinda like that.'

'I didn't say that.'

He nodded firmly. 'You did.'

She sighed in exasperation. 'It's not all about you, Riley.'

She didn't mean it quite to come out like that. But if he heard he didn't react badly. The smile was still plastered across his face. He must have thought she was joking with him.

If only that were true. Her heart gave a little squeeze.

If only she could have a different life. If only she could have a different gene pool. But that would mean that she and Mallory would never have existed—and she wouldn't have spent more than twenty years with a sister she'd both hated at times and adored. Sisterly love could never really be matched. And the bottom line was: she couldn't change her genes. She just had to find a way to manage her risk. For her, right now, that meant finding a way to live her life. She swallowed the huge lump in her throat. No matter what little strings were tugging at her heart right now, it was best to ignore them. Best to stay focused on what she could manage.

He glanced at his watch. 'I'm sorry to cut and run but I need to go and get Finn. I don't want to be late.' He pulled his jacket from the back of the chair. 'Thank you for your help with Finn. I mean it.' Then he gave her a cheeky wink. 'But it looks like I'm here to stay. Better get used to having me around.'

He disappeared out of the door into the snow as her heart gave a lurch.

Riley Callaghan here on a permanent basis.

This could be trouble.

CHAPTER FOUR

IN A WAY, the funeral went so much better than he ever could have expected.

The horrible conversation with Finn had turned out much easier than he could have hoped for. When April had come over to chat to Finn about flowers, Finn had asked outright if she would come to the funeral too.

It seemed that the thought of not being there hadn't even occurred to Finn.

Isabel's friends and workmates turned out in force. They all wore bright colours and sang along to the pop song that Finn had picked for his mum.

He was thankful they'd all attended. The decision to bury Isabel here instead of Birmingham had been a difficult one. But Riley and Finn would be the ones who tended her grave, and he didn't want to have to travel every time Finn wanted to visit.

April stayed steadily in the background. Finn had drawn her a picture of the flowers his mum liked best and, even though it was nearing the end of November, the church was full of orange gerbera daisies. The room felt bright. And Finn's little hand had gripped his the whole time.

He felt oddly detached about it all. He'd organised a funeral tea afterwards but only vaguely recognised a few of Isabel's friends, even though they all made a point of coming and speaking to Finn. The little guy seemed overwhelmed. April looked even more uncomfortable.

He crossed the room, Finn's hand still in his. He glanced down at Finn. 'I think we've probably stayed long enough. I was thinking we could do something together with Finn right now.'

He could tell she was hesitant but Finn had perked up at the suggestion. 'Can we go and pick a spaceman film?'

He looked at her again. She was pale in the black dress with her blonde hair tied back. The outfit had a severity to it that just didn't seem quite right for April. They'd discussed wearing something bright like Isabel's friends, but somehow it didn't feel quite right for them. April had found a brooch with a bright orange gerbera that matched the church flowers and pinned it to her dress. Riley had relented and worn a bright orange tie with his dark suit. Even though they'd asked Finn if he wanted to wear one of his superhero T-shirts he'd shaken his head; he'd wanted to wear a suit like his dad's.

Riley had been choked. He'd love to wear matching clothes with his son—just not like this. Everything about this was hard. He was questioning every decision he made.

He almost gave a shout when April gave a sigh of relief. 'Let me get my coat,' she said.

As they walked along the icy street together Finn reached out to hold April's hand too. Riley was glad of the cold, fresh air. Finn hadn't said much at all during the service. He'd placed a bunch of orange flowers by the grave and shed a few tears while Riley held him in his arms.

It had been exhausting. Smiling politely and shaking hands with people he really didn't know—all of whom he knew were looking him up and down and wondering about his suitability to bring up Finn.

He'd had a stand-up fight with his mother about

attending the funeral. She wanted to offer 'support' to her grandchild. But Riley had been insistent that the event was already too overwhelming for Finn. He'd been clear that she needed to wait a few days. Finn needed some space.

He would be starting full days at school next week and Riley had suggested his mum and dad come down to meet him then. He hadn't told her that Finn had video-chatted with his uncle Dan a few nights ago. It was obvious that Dan was smitten by his nephew straight away, and Finn with him, but Dan being away was actually easier. More manageable.

'Who is your favourite spaceman?' Finn asked April out of the blue.

She looked surprised and he could see her searching her brain. 'Well, it would have to be the one that I met.'

Finn stopped walking, his mouth hanging open. 'You've met a spaceman?'

She nodded. 'I went on holiday to Florida once and visited NASA. I got to have lunch with a spaceman. It was great.'

Finn's eyes were wide. 'Really? Dad, can we do that?'

Riley smiled. He was still getting used to being called Dad. First few times, he'd looked around to make sure it was really him that was being spoken to.

He gave a sort of nod. 'We haven't had a chance to talk about holidays yet. But it's always something we could consider.'

'Could we, Dad, could we?' The excitement on Finn's wide-eyed face made his heart swell. Right now he was tempted to promise the world to Finn, but he wasn't sure that was the best idea. He wanted his son to grow up to appreciate people, things and places. He was still trying to figure out everything in his head.

And that included the woman walking at the other side of his son.

April had been quiet most of the day. She'd agreed to come because Finn had asked her to. Riley wasn't sure she would have come on his invitation alone.

Although he'd been curious about April before, he hadn't pursued things. He'd been due to leave. But that hadn't stopped him trying to engage her constantly in conversation and trying to find out a little more about her.

Her face was serious. She'd told him she was good at funerals. She'd said she'd lost her sister but hadn't elaborated. Had today brought back some bad memories for her?

He was still curious about April. She was fantastic with patients. She'd been supportive to him in the most horrible set of circumstances. Even now, she was holding his son's hand. April Henderson had a good heart. Why didn't she let anyone get close to her?

They walked onto the main street and into one of the local shops. Finn raced over to the large display of DVDs. Riley put his hands in his pockets. 'Are you ready for this?'

She raised her eyebrows. 'You think I can't handle a little sci-fi?'

He gave a playful shrug. 'I thought you might be more of a romance girl.'

'Oh, no.' She shook her head straight away, even though her gaze was locked directly with his. A smile danced across her lips as she brushed past him to join Finn. 'What I don't know about *Star Wars*, *Star Trek* and Buzz Lightyear isn't worth knowing,' she whispered into his ear.

He grinned. Another tiny piece of information

about April Henderson. He was just going to keep chipping away at that armour she'd constructed around herself.

After a hard day for him and Finn, April was the brightest light on the horizon. And he'd never been so happy that she was there.

Two hours later Finn was fast asleep against April's shoulder. He might even have been drooling a little. The credits of the sci-fi movie were rolling on the screen. The room had grown dark and it was almost as if Riley read her mind as he crossed the room and flicked the switch on a lamp.

She wasn't quite sure how she'd managed to end up here. She hadn't intended to. But when Finn had asked her to come back she didn't have the heart to say no. Meaning that right now she had a five-year-old draped halfway across her, snoring.

Riley glanced towards her legs. As she'd sat on the sofa with Finn her dress had crept up a little more than it should. She tried to wiggle her dress down but it was nigh impossible with Finn's weight on top of her.

'April, can I get you something else a little more comfortable to wear?'

She almost laughed. It sounded like the old adage, *Do you want to slip into something more comfortable?*

He must have caught the expression on her face. 'I have scrubs,' he said quickly.

'Scrubs would be great,' she said. The black dress had been perfect for a funeral, but as the day had progressed it had started to feel more restrictive.

He disappeared for a second and set down a pale blue set of scrubs next to her, leaning over and adjusting Finn's position to free her up.

She pushed herself from the sofa and looked around. 'Bathroom this way?' she asked.

Riley nodded and she walked through to the hall. It was a typical army house. Adequate. But not perfect. As she wiggled out of her dress in the cramped bathroom she understood why he'd immediately thought about getting a place of his own. Everything in the house was bland. It would be difficult to put a stamp on the place and give it a family feel. It didn't really feel like a home.

By the time she came out of the bathroom,

Riley was in the kitchen. 'I thought I'd make us some dinner,' he said simply.

She opened her mouth to refuse straight away, then stopped. Would it really be so bad to share a meal with him? It had been a big day. For him, and for Finn. And, truth be told, for her too. It was the first funeral she'd been to since her sister's. It didn't help that Isabel had only been five years older than Mallory. Mallory's funeral had been full of young people too. And, while it was comforting, there was also a terrible irony about it. Some people were cheated out of the life they should live. If she was honest, she didn't really want to be alone right now.

'Can I help?'

Riley pulled a face. 'That depends.'

'On what?'

'On how fussy you are. I can make lasagne, spaghetti bolognaise or chilli chicken. That's as far as I can go.'

'Three things? I'm impressed. My speciality is chicken or sausage casserole.'

He laughed. 'Okay then, which of the five—' he opened his fridge '—no, sorry, four—I've no sausages—do you want to go for?'

April leaned her head on her hand. She was tired. It had been a long day. And it had been a long time since she'd had a conversation like this. A guy actually offering to make her dinner.

'I think I'm brave enough to try your lasagne. Do I get to watch the chef at work?'

He smiled. 'Sure you do. I'll even give you wine. But, just so you know, I'm a bit of a messy cook.'

He pulled two wine glasses out of the cupboard, held them up to the light and squinted at them. 'I'm just checking that they're clean. I moved in such a rush that I literally just walked from the flat to this house with things in my arms.'

She shook her head. 'Riley Callaghan. So far, you've told me that you only have three recipes, you're messy, and now I'm questioning your housekeeping skills.' She shook her head. 'If this were online dating, you wouldn't get a "like".'

He went into another cupboard and brought out two bottles. 'But I have wine! So I win. Now, white or red?'

'I guess for lasagne it should probably be red but I fancy white. Is that okay?'

He opened the bottle and poured the wine, then started pulling ingredients from the fridge.

She took a sip of the wine and relaxed back a little into the chair. 'I'll cut you a deal. You let me pick dinner—' she raised her eyebrows '—from a limited menu, of course, and you let me pick the wine. How about I do the clearing up?'

He tipped the mince into a pan to start browning it, giving her a wink from the corner of his eye. 'My plan has worked.'

April glanced back through to the living room at the little sleeping boy. 'Will Finn eat this?'

Riley followed her glance. 'Probably not. I'll give him it first, but have some chicken on standby in case he doesn't like it.' He leaned against the doorjamb as the mince began to sizzle in the pan. 'I wonder if he'll wake up at all. It's been a big day.' He picked up his glass and took a sip of his wine. 'Thanks for being there.'

She shrugged. 'It's fine. He's a cute kid.'

She could see the pride on his face. Riley was rapidly turning into a doting dad. He moved back into the kitchen and started chopping an onion.

He was methodical. He added the herbs and

tomatoes, then made a quick white sauce. Five minutes later he'd layered up the mix with lasagne sheets, sprinkled with cheese and put it in the oven.

She nodded. 'I'm impressed. You never struck me as the organised type.'

He sat down opposite her. 'I didn't? What's that supposed to mean?' He wrinkled his brow. 'Am I supposed to be offended right now? Because if I am, I'm just too tired.'

She shook her head. 'For the last four weeks you've been racing about the place doing one hundred things at once. The unit isn't normally like that.'

He pulled a face. 'I know.' He sat back a little and looked at her carefully. 'I've been used to working at a frantic pace. I need to step down a gear and get more perspective.'

'Can you actually do that?' she asked softly.

He sighed. 'I hate the way you do that.'

'What?'

He lifted his hand towards her. 'You ask the questions that I don't really want to answer.' He turned his head into the living room again. 'The answer to the question has to be yes. And you can see why. I have to change things. I have to be a father to Finn. I'm all he's got.'

'But…?'

He groaned and leaned forward, putting his head on the table. His real thoughts were written all over him. She touched his dark hair. 'You weren't born to be a rehab doctor, Riley. You want to be where the action is. But if you're going to have Finn on a permanent basis that will be impossible.'

He looked up a little as she shifted her hand, his bright green eyes peeking out from underneath dark lashes. 'I love him. I love him already. Finn comes first.'

She bent forward, her head almost touching his. 'You're allowed to say it, Riley. But maybe just to me. You're allowed to say that this life change gives you twinges of regret.' She licked her lips. 'Maybe I understand that a bit more than most.'

And she did. She was inches away from a guy a few years ago she would have flirted with, enjoyed his company and maybe even dated. There might even have been more possibilities that right now she didn't even dare think about.

His face crumpled and he put his head in his

hands for a second. He kept his eyes closed as he spoke. 'Last week I thought I was going on a tour of Sierra Leone. I was looking forward to it. It might sound strange but I love the overseas tours. Always have.' He opened his eyes slowly. 'But last week I didn't know I had a son to come home to. My whole life has changed in the blink of an eye. I'm not sure I was ready for it.'

She spoke carefully, sliding her hand across the table and letting her fingers intertwine with his. 'Promise me that you'll only ever talk to me about this. Don't let Finn know. You've had the legs swept from under you. Mallory and I used to call that being cannonballed. It will take a while to get your head around things. To work out what is best, for you and for him. You can do this, Riley. I know you can.'

He looked at their connected fingers. 'I'd never take out how I'm feeling on Finn. You must know that.'

'I do,' she said simply. 'But I want you to know that it's okay to feel like that. It's complicated. If you're having a bad day you can call me.'

They were touching. Having their fingers inter-twined was so much more personal than a brush of the hand. And it was sending a weird stream of little pulses up her arm. Under the bright kitchen lights there was nowhere to hide. Those bright green eyes were even more startling. Last time she'd seen something that green, she and Mallory had been taking a photo of the emerald-tinged sea in Zante at Shipwreck Beach. It was still one of her favourite ever pictures.

The little lines around his eyes gave him character, made her know that he'd seen and done things she never would. There was so much to like about Riley Callaghan, meaning there were so many more reasons to push him away.

So why wasn't she?

He looked at her, the barest hint of a smile quirking his lips. 'You mean you're going to give me your number?'

She frowned. 'Didn't I already when I was helping with the funeral arrangements?'

His fingers tightened around hers. 'Ah, but that was different. That was for practical reasons. This—' his smile broadened '—this sounds like almost *giving* a guy your number.'

She shook her head and pulled her hand back, surprised by how much she didn't want to. 'Don't get the wrong idea, mister.' She picked up her glass. 'You're supplying the wine and—' she nodded towards the oven '—the food. I'm a practical girl; I'm only nice as long as you're feeding me.'

Riley laughed. 'Oh, I have plenty of wine. As long as you're happy with a limited menu, we can be friends for ever.'

Something warm spread through her. It was like the kind of thing kids said to each other. The kind of thing she and Mallory used to say. Her fingers went automatically to her neck. To the pendant their parents had given both girls on their twenty-first birthdays. Two golden hearts linked together. Touching it made her feel closer to her sister. Touching it made her feel that sometimes Mallory wasn't quite as far away as reality told her.

'What's that? It's pretty.' Riley noticed her movement straight away.

She hesitated before letting her fingers fall away to reveal what she was touching. 'It was a gift from my parents.' She didn't add the rest.

Her brain started working overtime. What would Mallory have thought of Riley Callaghan? They'd generally had different taste in men. But somehow she knew Mallory would have loved this guy. It was both a comfort and a regret, that her sister wasn't here to meet him.

Riley leaned his head on his hands and gave her a curious stare. 'Are you going to tell me anything about yourself, April?'

She caught her breath. She hadn't expected him to be so direct. 'What do you mean?'

He counted off on his fingers. 'Well, I know you're a physio. I know you're a good physio—a great one. I'm not quite sure what age you are. Or where you live, although I know it's close. I know you had a sister. And you like spacemen.' He gave her a smile. 'But that's about it.'

She couldn't help but be defensive. 'What exactly do you think you're entitled to know about me?'

He stood up, his wooden chair scraping on the kitchen floor as he turned around, grabbed a tea towel and pulled the steaming-hot lasagne from the oven.

He didn't speak as he handed her a plate, some cutlery and a serving spatula. He didn't seem fazed by her briskness at all; in fact, it almost felt as if he was teasing her now. He sat down opposite and folded his hands on the table. 'I don't *think* I'm entitled to know anything. But I'd *like* it if you shared.' He even grinned. 'For example, my mum and dad are up north. My mother can best be described in terms of weather elements—she goes from snowstorm, sandstorm, whirlwind and tornado. My brother Dan is serving in the army. He's twenty-seven and can't wait to meet Finn. He probably is at the same stage of maturity.'

She wanted to smile. She really did. The waft of the enticing lasagne was winding its way across the table to her. He made everything sound so reasonable. But sharing wasn't the place she wanted to be right now. Sharing about her sister would mean sharing about the disease, and the follow-on questions about genetics. And surgery.

Inside, a little part of her shrivelled up and died. The whole reason she wasn't in a relationship right now was to give herself space to get this part of her life sorted. To not have to explain her thoughts or decisions to another person.

But a tiny part of her also recognised that she'd never actually been in a relationship where she would have been able to have that kind of serious conversation. Perhaps that was why she was trying to wrap Riley Callaghan up and stick him in a box somewhere in her brain before he let loose thoughts she wasn't ready for.

Thoughts like the ones where those perfectly formed lips were on hers.

She choked as Riley started to dish out the lasagne.

He still didn't speak. Just handed her the dish with a raise of his eyebrows.

This guy was too good at this.

'Maybe there's just not much to tell. I'm twenty-seven too. I've worked here for the last eighteen months. Before that I was in a general hospital, specialising in chronic injuries. And before that I did a year with kids who had cystic fibrosis. I've moved around to get a variety of experience.'

Not strictly true. She'd moved to the general hospital to be closer to Mallory when she'd got her diagnosis. And she'd moved to Waterloo Court after Mallory died because she couldn't face all the sympathy and questions from her colleagues. It was easier to be in a place where people didn't know your history.

'Are your mum and dad still around?'

She nodded. 'They moved up to Scotland just over a year ago. My nana was starting to get frail and they wanted to be closer to her.'

Her family felt as if it were falling apart. They'd lost one daughter and knew there was a possibility they could lose the other. And every time she looked at them she could see the pain in their eyes—that this was genetic. A time bomb that no one could have known about—at least not until fairly recently. But their pain had also affected her own decision. Would she want to risk passing faulty genes on to her own child? No. No way. Not when she saw the pain it could cause.

'Do you visit?'

She nodded. 'I visit a lot. Well, whenever I get time.' She looked up from the lasagne. 'I can't believe how good this is. Who taught you how to make it?'

He smiled. 'It's a secret.' His eyes were twinkling.

Was it a woman? She felt a tiny stab of envy.

He topped up her wine glass. 'I worked with an Italian doctor in an infectious disease unit for a while. He gave me his grandma's recipe.'

She kept eating. 'Well, I hate to say it, but

it might even beat my sausage casserole.' She glanced through to the living room. 'Do you want a hand to wrestle Finn into his pyjamas? I don't think he's going to wake up now.'

Riley followed her gaze as he kept eating. 'In a minute. Darn it—jammies. I need to put them on the list.'

'Finn doesn't have pyjamas?'

He shook his head. 'He does, but I think he might just have taken a little stretch. Either that or I've shrunk them in the wash. I'll need to get him some new ones.' He looked around the plain kitchen. 'And I need to get some decorations too. I don't even own a Christmas tree. I'm not even sure where to buy one around here.'

'There's a place just a few miles out of town— that's if you want a real one, of course. They can be a little messy, but they smell great.'

'Will you show me?'

She paused. She wanted to say no. She should say no. But a little bit inside of her wanted to say yes. Riley Callaghan was messing with her mind.

'I can give you directions.'

'I didn't ask for directions.' His fork was poised in mid-air and he was looking at her pointedly.

She licked her lips. It didn't matter she'd had plenty of wine; all of a sudden her mouth felt very dry. 'Why don't we just play it by ear? I've got some plans in the next few days. If you let me know when you're going I can see if I'm free.'

His eyes narrowed for a moment. He was a doctor. He could recognise a deflected question easily. It was second nature. But Riley was gracious enough not to push.

They finished dinner and she washed up while he prepared Finn's room. It only took a few minutes to wiggle Finn into his pyjamas, and then Riley carried him up to bed.

She couldn't help but follow him up the stairs as he laid Finn down in his bed adorned with a spaceman duvet. He whispered in his son's ear, put a kiss on his forehead and switched on the nightlight that illuminated stars on the ceiling.

'Oh, wow,' whispered April. 'That's fantastic.' She smiled at him in the dim light. 'I think I want one.'

He raised his eyebrows as he walked back to the doorway, his shoulder touching hers as he bent to whisper, 'I hate to break it to you, but you'll have to sweet-talk my mother. She sent it down yesterday for Finn and I've no idea where she got it.'

April watched the circling stars on the ceiling. It was almost magical. Hypnotic. And by the time she stopped watching she'd forgotten about how close she was to Riley. She could smell his aftershave. Smell the soap powder from the soft T-shirt he'd changed into when they'd got home. Her eyes fixed on the rise and fall of his chest, then the soft pulse at the base of his neck. She was suddenly conscious that the scrubs she was wearing were thin. Thin enough to probably see the outline of her black matching underwear beneath the pale blue fabric.

All of a sudden it felt as though a part of life that was so far out of reach was right before her eyes. A gorgeous man, a beautiful child—things she couldn't even contemplate. Things that seemed so far away and unobtainable. When she and Mallory had been young they'd always joked about who would marry first, and being each other's bridesmaids. They'd both taken it for granted that those things would naturally happen. Right now, she had to concentrate on surgery. Getting through that, gaining a little confidence again and getting some normality back to her life. Pursuing anything with Riley Callaghan wasn't possible. It wasn't fair to her. It wasn't fair to him. It especially wasn't fair to a little boy whose whole world had just been turned upside down.

In the dim light Riley's hand lifted oh-so-slowly towards her. 'April—'

She turned swiftly and walked out of the room, her breath catching somewhere in the back of her throat. She needed to go. She needed to get out of there.

She rushed down the stairs and picked up the bag with her dress in it and her black coat. 'It's getting late. I need to get home. Thanks for dinner.' She said the words far too brightly.

Riley was at her back, but his hands were in his pockets and his eyes were downcast. 'Yeah. No problem. Thanks for coming today. I appreciate it.'

She nodded as she slipped her arms into her jacket and headed for the door. 'Say goodnight to Finn for me. See you at work tomorrow.'

Riley gave the briefest of nods as she hurried out the door. It didn't matter how quickly she walked, she could sense his eyes searing into her back the whole way, as the smell of his aftershave still lingered around her.

He watched as she hurried away like a scalded cat. What had he done? He hadn't *actually* touched her. Yes, he'd meant to. Yes, he'd wanted to.

His lips were still tingling from the fact he'd wanted to kiss her. To let his lips connect with hers. Right now, he almost felt cheated.

But it was clear that something else was going on.

There was a reason he'd been curious about April Henderson. It wasn't the good figure, the blonde hair and cute smile. It was *her*. The way she engaged with the patients. The way he could tell sometimes she was considering things, trying to do what was best. She'd captured his attention in a way he'd never really been caught before.

She'd relaxed a little around him tonight. When she'd been with Finn she'd been happy. She was so good around Finn. He seemed to almost sparkle when he was with her they connected so well.

And it wasn't just Finn. Riley wasn't imagining

things. There was definitely something in the air between them. Even though she was trying her best to ignore it.

He should probably ignore it too. Finn was his priority. Christmas was coming. His son was about to face his first Christmas without his mother, but Riley was about to spend the first Christmas with his son.

He wasn't even sure how to mark the occasion. He should be overjoyed and happy, but in the circumstances it wasn't appropriate.

There were obvious times when Finn's childhood innocence shone through. He spoke about his mum. He cried at times. But children possessed a resilience that adults couldn't quite comprehend. And he seemed to be settling in to his new house, his new surroundings.

But for Riley there was something else. Finn seemed to light up around April. It seemed he'd spent much of his five years around women, so that didn't seem so unusual.

What was unusual was the way it made Riley's heart skip a beat.

Or two.

He sighed and closed the door. It was just the

wrong time. He still had to work out his career plans. His house plans.

His life plans.

It was best that he do it alone.

CHAPTER FIVE

WORK FELT STRANGE. April had spent most of the last few days glancing over her shoulder in an attempt to try to stay out of Riley's way.

What might have happened if she'd stayed longer the other night? It annoyed her that there was almost an ache inside at the mere thought of it. By the time she'd got home that night she'd been resolute. It was best not to get involved with Riley and Finn Callaghan. Things would get busy anyhow. They would forget about her. Riley's parents would visit and Christmas plans would start to be made. She could fade into the background and take care of herself for now.

So why had she spent the last few days with her stomach doing flip flops?

Lucy, the staff nurse in the ward, was waiting for her when she arrived. 'Hi, April. You here to see John Burns?'

April nodded. John had been wounded in action

and after a few weeks with an extremely damaged lower leg and a persistent infection they'd taken the decision to perform an amputation. 'How's he doing?'

Lucy pushed his notes over. 'Riley's spent quite a bit of time with him this morning. He's had a lot of phantom pain. He had some analgesia about two hours ago, so he should be fit for you to see.'

She nodded and walked down the corridor towards John's room. She could hear the laughter before she reached the room and her footsteps faltered. Riley. This was where he'd been hiding out. From the way Lucy had spoken she'd assumed that Riley had already left.

She screwed up her face. She couldn't avoid this. It was her job. Physiotherapy was essential for John's recovery and for his confidence. She'd just have to keep her professional face in place.

She fixed on a smile and walked into the room. 'Good morning, John. How are you doing today?'

Riley was sitting on an easy chair in the corner of the room. He looked comfortable. Too comfortable. She gave him a glance. 'We don't want you distracting us, Dr Callaghan. John and I have some work to do.'

John was sitting up on the bed. He waved his hand. 'No, it's fine. Riley wanted to stay to make sure I'm good to go with the painkillers he's given me.' John shook his head. 'I just can't get my head around this phantom pain stuff. How can I feel something that just isn't there?'

April took a deep breath. Riley hadn't spoken; he was just watching her with those green eyes. She turned her full attention to John as she sat beside his bed. 'You're right. It is difficult to understand. And we still don't really know why it happens. Scientists think that the sensations come from the spinal cord and brain. The imprint of the leg has always been there, so it's almost like the brain keeps hold of it.' She licked her lips. 'You're not alone, John. Lots of patients experience phantom pain after this kind of operation. It's our job to manage that pain for you. So you need to tell me if anything we do today is too uncomfortable.'

John let out a sigh. 'I just want to get back on my feet as soon as possible.' Then he realised the irony of his statement. He let out a hollow laugh. 'Well, at least one of them.' He met April's gaze. 'I just want to get some normality back. The last few months have been terrible. I want to be able to do things for myself.'

April nodded in appreciation. John's mobility had been badly affected by his damaged and infected limb; that had been part of the decision for the amputation. 'And we'll get you there, John. We will.'

She looked at his position. 'How has lying flat worked out for you?'

The first essential procedure for patients who'd had an amputation was to lie flat for at least an hour each day. This helped straighten the hip as much as possible. Any risk of hips tightening could make it more difficult to walk with a prosthesis.

John gave a nod. 'That's been okay.'

She gave him a smile. 'So how do you feel about hitting the gym with me today?'

He grinned. 'I thought you'd never ask. Music to my ears.'

She wheeled in the chair that was parked in the corridor outside, taking care to help him change position and ease into it. Riley stood up.

She gave him a tight smile. 'I take it you have

other patients to see? I can leave a report for you about how John does in the gym.'

But it seemed that the more she tried to brush off Riley, the more determined he became. And the most annoying thing about that was how casual he was about it. He didn't act offended. He didn't appear to be angry. He just seemed determined to hang around.

She pushed John down the corridor to the state-of-the-art gym. It was specially designed for patients with spinal cord injuries and amputations. April turned towards Riley. If he was going to hang around, she might as well use him.

'I've looked over John's wound and think it's looking good. Good enough to take part in a walking trial. What do you think?'

Riley nodded. 'It's healing well. No problems. I think it would be useful to see how John manages.'

April gave a nod and took the chair closer to the parallel walking bars. She turned around and picked up what she'd left in preparation for today's session. 'We're going to try one of these,' she said, smiling as she watched the expression on John's face.

'What on earth is that?'

She kept smiling. 'It's called a pam aid. Pneumatic Post-Amputation Mobility Aid. It's basically an inflatable leg. It helps reduce the swelling around your stump and helps you walk again. We need to assess your muscle strength and standing tolerance.' She raised her eyebrows. 'And the big one—your balance.' She gestured behind her. 'We always start with the parallel bars.'

John frowned. 'Can't you just give me one of those prosthetic limbs and let me get on with it?'

Riley stood up alongside as April started to make adjustments to John's stump-shrinker compression sock. 'If you manage well with your walking trial over the next few days then we'll make arrangements to have you fitted with a prosthetic limb. But it has to be made just for you. And we have to wait until your wound is completely healed and any residual swelling has gone down.'

John gave a nod. 'Then let's get started. I want to be out of this wheelchair as soon as I can be.'

It was almost like being under the microscope. Even though she knew Riley was there to observe John, every move she made, every conversation that she started felt a little forced. She hadn't even been this self-conscious when she was a student and was being assessed.

Riley, on the other hand, seemed completely at ease. He cracked jokes with John and kept him distracted while April got things ready.

But she was conscious of the way he watched. It was annoying. Her emotions were heightened.

Eventually she stopped keeping the false smile on her face. 'Are you going to do something to actually help?'

Riley's brow furrowed with a deep frown. Now, finally, he looked annoyed. He glanced around the gym as he positioned himself next to John. 'What would you like me to do?'

April pulled herself into professional mode. It was the safest place to be. Then she wouldn't notice those eyes. Then she wouldn't focus on the fresh smell stretching across the room towards her.

She didn't even look at him. She waved her hand. 'I'll stay on one side of John. You stay on the other.'

She bent forward in front of John. 'First time standing on your own can be difficult. I'm going to let you push yourself up—it's best if you can get a sense of your own balance without us taking your weight. Don't worry. If it's too painful, we can help you sit back down, and we're on either side; we won't let you fall.'

John nodded. Guys who'd served always had a grim determination about every task. They didn't like to fail at anything and John was no different. He placed a hand on either parallel bar and pulled himself up sharply. April kept her hands off but close by, ready to catch him if he swayed. There was a kind of groan. Weight bearing on a stump for the first time would be sending a whole new range of sensations about John's body. She didn't look up at Riley. He had adopted a similar position to herself, ready to take the strain of John's weight if it were necessary.

After around thirty seconds, John's breathing started to slow a little. 'Okay,' he said gruffly. 'It's not exactly comfortable, but it's bearable.' He turned his head to April. 'Do I get to walk in this thing?'

She nodded. 'Only a few steps at a time. I'm going to pull the wheelchair behind us so it's handy if you need it.'

John shook his head. 'No way. I'm going to make it to the end of these bars.'

She smiled. Somehow she didn't doubt he would.

Riley leaned forward. 'John, just remember. This isn't a military operation. Your wound is healing well. But parts will still hurt. We need to be able to judge how much analgesia you need to be able to take part in your physical therapy. If we give you too much, you could do yourself harm. Push your body to do things it's not quite ready for.'

'Do people normally make it to the end of the bars?' John asked April.

She held up her hands. 'Some people can't weight bear at all the first time. Some people can stand for a few minutes; others manage a few steps. We're all individuals, John. And this is the first day. Your first steps. Let's just take it as it comes.'

He nodded, his hands gripping tightly to the bars, his knuckles blanching.

She could see Riley noticing the same things that she was. Why was he even here? This was her job. Doctors rarely visited the gym. They usually only appeared if their presence was requested.

Suddenly, there was a pang in her stomach and she caught her breath. That had been a few times today. She hoped she wasn't coming down with something.

John took a step forward with his affected leg. She pressed her lips together for the next stage. It was just as she expected. He had his weight on the amputated limb for the briefest of seconds before his weight fell back on his good leg.

That was entirely normal. It was hard for the body to adjust. It was hard for the brain to make sense of the changes. John was starting to sweat. It was amazing how much work just a few steps could take. She stayed right next to him. As did Riley.

It took another ten minutes to reach the end of the parallel bars. By the time John had finished he was thankful to sink back down into the wheelchair. April put her hands on his shoulders. 'Well done, John. That was great.' She walked around to the front to release the pam aid. 'Ideally, we'll do a bit of work in the gym three times a day.' She looked at Riley. 'Dr Callaghan will have a conversation with you about what works best analgesia-wise for you. The more regularly we can get you down to the gym, the more quickly your body and brain will adjust. The nurses will also do regular checks of your wound to make sure there are no problems.'

John gave an exhausted sigh. 'Any chance of a coffee?'

She laughed. 'Absolutely.' She set the pam aid aside. 'I'll take you back down to the ward and we'll set a programme for tomorrow.'

John looked over at Riley. 'She's a hard task-master.'

Riley's voice wasn't as relaxed as it had been earlier. 'She is. But it's the only way to get you back on your feet.'

He pushed his hands into his pockets as April finished tidying up. His pager sounded and he glanced at it. The expression on his face changed.

'Sorry, need to go.' He'd already started striding down the corridor in front of them when he turned around and looked back. 'John, I'll be back to talk to you later.'

April watched his retreating back. Part of her

wanted to ask what was wrong. Part of her knew it was none of her business.

Could something be wrong with Finn?

She tried to push things out of her mind. She had a patient to look after. She had work to do. But, as they reached John's room, he said the words she'd dreaded. 'Isn't Ballyclair the local school?'

She nodded.

'Thought so. That's what his pager said. Hope his kid is okay.'

Her footsteps faltered as she took the final steps towards the chair in John's room. 'Oops, sorry!' she said brightly as she bent down to put on the brake. Her heart was thudding against her chest. She moved automatically, helping John into the other chair.

This was none of her business. None of her business at all.

So why did she want to pull her mobile from her pocket and phone Riley right now?

One of the nurses stuck her head around the door. 'April, are you free? I'm wondering if I could steal you to do some chest physio on someone who is sounding a little crackly?'

She nodded straight away. Work—that was what she had to do. That was what she should be concentrating on. She smiled at John. 'Can we coordinate our diaries for around two p.m. and we can go back to the gym again?'

John put his hand on his chin. 'Let me think. There's the afternoon movie. Or the browsing of the dating websites. But I think I can fit you in.'

She laughed and put her hand on his shoulder. 'You did good this morning. Let's keep working hard. See you in a while.'

Her fingers brushed against her phone again and she pulled them from her pocket.

None of her business.

She gritted her teeth and kept walking.

He was trying to be rational. But the words 'Finn's been hurt' had sent a deep-rooted fear through him that he'd never experienced before. His legs had just started walking to the car even with the phone still pressed to his ear.

Apparently it was 'just a little head-knock'. When was any head injury 'just a little head-knock'? Finn had slid in the school playground, fallen backwards, cracked his head on the concrete and been knocked out for a few seconds.

His car was eating up the road in front of him. Finn's school was only a ten-minute drive from the hospital but right now it felt like a million miles away.

His mum and dad had come down for the weekend to meet Finn. He'd told April that his mum was like a whirlwind—truth was she'd been more like a tornado. She'd taken over everything. Cooking. Cleaning. Every conversation with Finn. His dad had been much more thoughtful. But Riley could tell that his father just wanted a chance to have five minutes to sit down with his grandson.

It hadn't helped that his mother kept bursting into tears every now and then. Finn had just seemed a little bewildered by it all. He'd finall whispered to Riley, 'I've never had a gran before,' as he'd watched Riley's mum talk and cook at a hundred miles an hour. Riley had given him a hug.

It had all been exhausting. His mother hadn't wanted to leave, and Riley had been forced to tell her quite pointedly that he needed some time with his son. Right now, he was regretting that decision. What if he needed some help with Finn?

His eyes narrowed as he noticed the traffic slowing in front of him on the motorway. He'd come this way to save a few minutes and to stop wasting time at a hundred sets of traffic lights in the town. Seemed like it hadn't been the best plan.

His foot hit the brake as it became clear that things were much worse than he could ever imagine. Smoke was directly ahead. The cars in front had stopped, but it was clear the accident had only happened around thirty seconds before.

Riley's stomach clenched. Two cars, both totally smashed, facing each other and blocking the motorway completely.

For the first time in his life he was completely torn. His doctor instincts told him to get out of the car and start helping. But his newly honed parental instincts told him to find a way to Finn.

He gulped and looked behind him. It only took a few minutes for the motorway to back up completely. There was no exit nearby. There was no way out of here.

He pulled his phone from his pocket as he

climbed out of the car. Someone else had already jumped out and ran to the smoking cars. For the first time he regretted sending his mother back home after her weekend meeting Finn. There was only one other natural person to phone in a situation like this. He pressed her name on the screen as he opened the boot of his car and grabbed the emergency kit that he always kept there.

There was only one other person he'd trust with Finn.

April's stomach plummeted when she saw who was calling. 'Riley? What's wrong? Is it Finn? Is he okay?'

His voice was eerily calm. But she could hear some shouting in the background. 'April? There's an accident on the motorway. I can't get off. And I need to help. The school phoned. Can you get Finn? Can you check he's okay? He's had a head injury. He was knocked out. Don't come this way. You'll have to drive through the town. Check his reactions. Check his pupils. If he's nauseous or sleepy take him to hospital.'

April was stunned. It took a few seconds to find some words.

'Of…of course. Of course I'll get Finn. No problem. Riley, are you okay?'

She could almost physically feel his pause. 'I'm fine. I have to go and help. Just take care of Finn.'

She stared at the phone. Her hand had the slightest shake. April moved into automatic pilot. She wasn't sure if Riley had spoken to anyone when he'd left, so she followed procedures and spoke to her boss, making arrangements for someone to cover her workload, and then left a message for Riley's boss. Waterloo Court was a real family-friendly place. No one had problems about her leaving. It only took fifteen minutes to drive through town and reach the school.

Finn was sitting at the office as she arrived, looking a little pale-faced. He didn't seem surprised to see her as she rushed over to sit next to him and give him a hug.

The head teacher looked at her in surprise. She held out her hand in a way that only a head teacher could. 'I'm Mrs Banks. I don't believe we've met. I was expecting Dr Callaghan.'

April nearly opened her mouth to speak, then had a wave of realisation. She pointed through the doors. 'Can we speak in there, please?' She didn't wait for a reply before she whispered in Finn's ear, 'I'll be just a second, honey.'

Once they'd walked through the doors she held out her hand to the head teacher. 'Apologies. I'm April Henderson. I'm a colleague of Dr Callaghan. He's stuck at a road accident on the motorway. I didn't want to say that in front of Finn, since he lost his mother in an accident.'

The head teacher gave a nod of acknowledgement and shook April's hand. 'Of course. I understand. But we have a problem.'

'We do?'

She nodded. 'I'm afraid Dr Callaghan hasn't named you as an emergency contact. It means I can't let you take Finn away.'

'Oh.' It was all she could say. Her brain filled with distant memories of conversations with colleagues over the years about making things safer for kids at school. Of course they wouldn't just hand Finn over to anyone. But that hadn't even occurred to her on the way there. It must not have occurred to Riley either. They were both treading waters unknown.

'I take it Riley didn't manage to call you and

tell you I was coming?' Why did she even ask that? Of course not. She shook her head. 'He's treating people at the accident scene.'

The head teacher gave her best sympathetic look. 'Well, I'm sorry. But we have good reasons for our rules. Until we hear from Dr Callaghan, we can't let you leave with Finn.'

April glanced through the glass panel in the door, where Finn was so white he seemed transparent. She took a deep breath. 'Let me keep trying to get hold of Riley while I keep an eye on Finn.'

Riley surveyed the scene. Two cars—both had their bonnets completed crumpled, one had its side doors crushed inwards. He ran towards the cars, checking in one, then the other. Another man was talking to a lady in the first car.

'I'm Riley Callaghan, a doctor.'

The guy looked up. 'I'm Phil—just Phil. I know a little first aid but that's it.'

Riley gave a nod and took a quick look in the car. It was an elderly couple. The man was unconscious, the woman making a few groans. Both looked trapped by the crumpled front end of the car. Riley tried to pull the door open nearest to him. After a few attempts he put his foot up to get more leverage. The door opened but not completely. He put his hand in and felt for a pulse, watching the rise and fall of the man's chest. He grabbed some gloves from his back pocket—life had taught him to permanently have them handy. He then put his hand down the non-existent footwell. He fumbled around. There was no way to see clearly, but after a few seconds he found a pulse at one ankle, but couldn't get to the other. He pulled out his hand; unsurprisingly the glove was covered in blood. He pulled it off and found another. 'How's she doing?' he asked Phil.

Phil pulled a face. 'I'm not sure.'

Riley was around the car in an instant. 'Mind if I have a look?'

Phil stepped out of the way. Riley was keeping calm; his main aim was to have assessed the occupants of both cars in as short a time as possible. He'd take it from there.

He checked the woman's pulse. She was terribly pale, but that might be her normal colour. He checked her breathing; it was erratic and he put his hand gently at her chest. She'd broken some ribs. He was sure of it. And it could be that one had pierced her lung. He did a quick check of her legs. One was definitely broken; he suspected both tib and fib. The second seemed okay.

'Stay with her,' he said. 'I'm going to check the other car.'

He crossed quickly to the other car. There was a man of a similar age to him, coughing, with a little blood running down his forehead. The airbag had deployed and the air was still a little clouded around him. The man was clearly dazed. In between coughs he spluttered, 'Aaron. How's Aaron?'

Riley felt his heart plummet. He looked into the back of the car. A little boy—around two—was strapped into a car seat. He yanked at the rear car door, pulling it with all his might. It was stiff. Part of the door was buckled, but after some tugging he finally pulled it free. The little boy greeted him with a big smile. He started babbling and wiggling his legs.

Riley's actions were automatic. This car already had smoke coming from the engine. He reached and unclipped the little guy, grabbing him with both hands and pulling him out. He leaned Aaron towards his father. He would never have thought to do something like that before. But he could see that in amongst his confused state the man's first thoughts had been for his son.

Finn. As held the little body next to his, all he could think about was Finn. Was he okay? Had April got to him yet? He should be with him. Not here.

Not stuck at a roadside.

'Aaron looks good; the car seat has kept him protected.' He glanced anxiously at the man as his head slumped forward a little. It was obvious he was still completely dazed. 'What's your name?'

'Ben,' came the mumbled reply.

'Well, Ben, I'm going to hand Aaron over to someone else to keep an eye on him and get him somewhere safe. We need to think about getting you out of this car.'

A woman had appeared from one of the cars stranded in the traffic jam. She arrived just as he turned around. He moved away from the cars. 'Can you hold this little guy for a second?' She held out her hands and Riley thrust Aaron into them. 'Wait a second,' he commanded and he gave Aaron a quick check over. No apparent injuries. Breathing fine. Moving all limbs. No abrasions. He pulled his pen torch from his back pocket, choking back a gulp. He'd meant to use this on Finn. He quickly checked Aaron's pupils. Both equal and reacting to light.

He looked at the woman. 'This is Aaron. Everything looks fine but can you take him over to the side of the road and keep an eye on him for now?'

She nodded quickly, seeming relieved to be of some help. 'No problem.' She started chatting to Aaron as she walked away. Riley's phone rang.

April.

He actually thought he might be sick. Something must be wrong with Finn. It must be something terrible. A subdural haematoma? Skull fracture? Intracranial bleeding? His hand fumbled with the phone. 'April? What's wrong?'

'Riley. Are you okay? Finn looks fine. But the school won't let me take him home. They say they need permission.'

Relief flooded through him, rapidly followed by frustration. 'Let me speak to them.' He turned back to the car. The smoke looked a little worse. He needed to get Aaron's dad out of there.

A stern voice appeared on the phone. 'Dr Callaghan? Mrs Banks, head teacher. I'm afraid you haven't listed Ms Henderson as an emergency contact for Finn. We really need you to sign some paperwork so that, like today, we can release Finn into her care.'

He was instantly annoyed. He knew why Mrs Banks was saying all this, but it felt like a reprimand for an unruly child. As he stood, flames started licking from the silver car holding Aaron's dad. 'Damn it!' He started running back towards the car. He tucked the phone under his chin, put his foot on the car and started pulling at the driver's door with all his might. 'Come on!' he yelled in frustration at the door.

'What?' came a squeak from the phone.

'Mrs Banks,' he said between yanks at the door. 'I'm trying to pull a guy from a burning car. You—' he stopped and pulled again '—have my permission to—' every muscle in his arms was starting to ache '—release Finn into April's custody.' He pushed the phone away from his ear and shouted to some guys who were talking near the front of the traffic jam. 'Can you give me some help over here?' He could feel the heat from the flames near the bare skin on his arms. He pushed the phone back to his ear. 'Could you do that, please?'

He pushed the phone back into his pocket, not bothering to wait for a reply. April was there. She'd seen Finn. She'd said he was okay. Maybe his definition of okay was different from hers, but he had to have faith in his colleague. Had April worked with kids before? Hadn't she mentioned something about kids with cystic fibrosis? Maybe she knew more than he thought.

Three men ran over; one joined him, two tried the opposite side of the car. Why hadn't he thought of that?

The man's hands squished over his at the handle. 'Now,' he grunted at Riley as the two of them pulled in unison. His hands were nearly crushed beneath the guy's vice-like grip but the extra strength gave him what he needed. The car door was finally prised open and they both landed on the ground.

Riley picked himself up and leaned in to check on Ben just as the flames shot up towards the sky.

The two men on the other side of the car yelled and leapt backwards. Riley reached forward to check Ben's legs weren't trapped. He knew the rules. A casualty should never be moved from a vehicle without a neck collar in place to protect them.

But threat of imminent death from fire took priority over all the normal rules.

He gestured to the other guy. 'Give me a hand getting him out of here.' There was a sound of sirens in the distance. The other guy looked at the flames. Riley could see the doubt on his face but, to his credit, the guy stood up and came forward. Together, they half pulled, half lifted Ben out of the car, looping arms around his waist and carrying him over to the side of the road.

Ben winced in pain as Riley touched his leg. Riley glanced around. His emergency bag was lying on the ground next to the first car. He ran and picked it up, pulling a swab out to stem the bleeding from Ben's forehead.

He shouted over to Phil, whom he'd left at the side of the first car. 'How's everything?'

Phil looked anxious. 'Her lips look a bit blue,' he shouted back.

Riley looked up. He could see the blue flashing lights now and the sirens were getting louder. The police cars and ambulances were trying to weave their way through the traffic. They would still be a few minutes.

He ran over to the car to check both patients again. A quick glance at the man showed he still hadn't regained consciousness. But his pulse was strong and he was breathing easily. The leg injuries remained but it was likely that he'd need to be cut out of the car. There wasn't much Riley could do for him at the side of the road. He turned his attention back to the woman. He spoke quietly. Her handbag was behind the seat, so he checked her details. 'Elizabeth? Mrs Bennett?' She gave a nod. 'I'm Riley. I'm a doctor. There's an ambulance coming soon.' He put his fingers on her pulse again. It was faster and more thready than before. 'Are you having difficulty breathing?'

She nodded again. He glanced at Phil at the other side of the car. 'Take a run towards the ambulance. Tell them we have a pneumo—' He changed his mind about the language. 'Tell them a possible punctured lung. Tell them I need some oxygen.'

Phil nodded and took off. The cars were doing their best to get out of the way of the police cars and ambulances but there was virtually no room to manoeuvre.

Riley was frustrated. He hated the fact he had little or no equipment. From her colour, Mrs Bennett had either a collapsed lung or a blood-filled one. Both needed rapid treatment. But there was nothing he could do right now. He held her hand and spoke quietly to her, trying to ascertain if she had family and if there was someone to contact, in case she became too unwell to communicate. The thud of boots behind him made him look up. The familiar green overalls of a paramedic. He was carrying as much equipment as he could. His eyes fixed on the car that was now firmly alight.

'Tell me no one is in that?'

Riley shook his head. 'Man and a little boy, both at the side of the road. They'll need to be checked but—' he nodded to the car '—Mr and Mrs Bennett look as if they need attention first.'

The paramedic nodded. 'Eric' was his reply. 'What we got?' He handed over the oxygen cylinder.

'Lieutenant Riley Callaghan, a doctor at Waterloo Court.' He leaned forward. 'Elizabeth, I'm just going to slip an oxygen mask over your face.' He did that quickly. 'Mr and Mrs Bennett. Mr Bennett has been unconscious since I got here. I think he has a fractured tib and fib in the footwell. His pulse has been strong and his breathing fine. Mrs Bennett, I think, may have had some damage from the seat belt and I don't know about her pelvis. She also looks like she has a tib and fib fracture. I think she may have fractured a few ribs and punctured a lung.'

A female paramedic arrived too, shaking her head. 'Still can't get the ambulances through. Where do you want me?'

Eric signalled to the side of the road where Aaron and his dad were sitting and she nodded and ran over. Eric ripped open the large pack he'd brought with him. 'Right, Doc, let's get to work.'

CHAPTER SIX

FINN WAS SLEEPING NOW. April wasn't quite sure
what Riley had said to Mrs Banks on the phone,
but Finn had been released into her care with a
few mutterings of 'exceptional circumstances'.

After she'd realised she didn't have a key to
Riley's place, she'd made a quick trip to the
shops to let Finn pick something for dinner then
brought him back to her flat.

Thank goodness for the TV. There was a whole
host of kids' TV channels she'd never known
about or watched, but Finn could tell her exactly
where to find them. She'd checked him over as
best she could and, apart from being a little pale
and not wanting to eat much, he seemed fine.
As soon as he'd eaten a little dinner, he'd fallen
asleep, lying on the sofa with a cover over him.

Part of her had been nervous. Hadn't Riley said
something about sleepiness being a sign of head
injury? But her gut instincts told her that Finn

was simply exhausted. It was after seven; she wasn't sure when he normally went to bed.

She walked through to the kitchen to make herself a drink but when she came back through Finn was awake again with his nose pressed up against the window.

'Hey,' she said gently as she crossed the room and put an arm on his shoulder. 'What are you looking at?'

It took her a second or two to realise his shoulders were shaking a little. She knelt down beside him so she could see his face. 'Finn? What's wrong?'

'I… I heard someone shouting. I heard someone shouting my name…' His voice stalled for a second.

April glanced outside. There was a family directly under her window, laughing and carrying on in the light dusting of snow outside. The woman shouted at the little boy and girl. 'Finn, Jessie, come over here.'

Finn started to shake next to her. 'I thought it was my mum,' he gasped. 'I thought it was her.'

Her actions were instinctive. She gathered the little body as Finn's legs collapsed under him and he started to sob. She pulled him in towards her shoulder and stood up, clutching him tightly. Normally she would have thought a five-year-old might be too big to carry like a toddler. But there was nothing else she could do right now. Finn needed her and she would never let him down.

She rubbed his back as he sobbed and whispered in his ear. 'I'm so sorry, honey. I'm so sorry that your mum isn't here.'

His words came out in gasps. 'I… I…miss… her.'

Tears started to flow down her face. She walked over to the sofa and sat down, keeping Finn firmly in her arms. 'I know you do. Of course you do. And I know that your mum wishes she was still here with you.'

He curled in her arms, pulling up his knees and resting his head on her chest. 'I want my mum.'

She rocked back and forward. His pain was so raw. So real. She wanted to reach out and grab it. To take it away for him. No child should have to go through this.

She stroked his hair. 'It's not the same. But I had a sister who died not long ago. I know how hard it is when you lose someone you love very much. And it is hard, Finn. I won't tell you lies. You'll miss your mum every single day. And while it's really horrible right now, and you'll think about her all the time, I promise that at some point it won't be quite as bad as it is now.'

Finn shook his head. 'I just want her back. I just want to go home.'

It was almost like a fist reaching inside and twisting around her heart.

She kept rocking. 'I know you do, honey. But you're going to have a new home with your dad. He loves you. He loves you just as much as your mum does. It just takes a little getting used to. For him too.' She gave a little sigh and tried to find the right words. Were there even right words?

'Mum used to do this,' whispered the little voice.

April froze mid-rock.

She'd only done what came naturally. She wasn't trying to be a mum to Finn. She was just doing what she thought she should.

Finn's hand crept up and his finger wound in her hair. Now, it was her turn to almost shake. 'Can we stay like this till I fall asleep?' came the tired voice.

Her brain was screaming silent messages at her. *No! Too close.*

Her body started to rock again, but she couldn't say the words out loud. It was almost like being on automatic pilot. And even though her movements were steady her thoughts weren't.

She was overstepping the mark. This was wrong. It was Riley's job to comfort his son— not hers. She couldn't let Finn rely on her. That would be wrong. That would be *so* wrong. Particularly when she didn't know what might lie ahead.

Finn's little heart had already been broken once. It was bad enough for a child to experience that once. If things developed…

She pushed the thoughts straight from her head. No. They wouldn't. She couldn't let them. It wasn't good for her. And it really wasn't good for Finn.

Her brain buzzed as she kept rocking until the little finger released its grip on her hair and Finn's head sagged to the side.

Moving carefully, she positioned him on the sofa with a blanket on top as she stood on the other side of the room, leaning against the wall and breathing heavily.

She hadn't meant for this to happen. She was getting too close. She was feeling too much.

A few extra tears slid down her cheeks. She had to get a hold of herself.

But it wasn't how he felt about her that was hardest. It was how she felt about him, and Riley.

For her, they were a perfect combination at a completely imperfect time. A guy who made her heart beat quicker with just one glance, and a little boy with so much love to give.

Her heart ached. She just wasn't ready for this. Not right now.

There was a gentle knock at the door. It startled her and she took a few deep breaths, pushing her hair back from her face and wiping her eyes before she pulled it open.

Riley looked exhausted. He was still wearing his pale blue scrubs from work. They were rumpled and had a number of stains that she really didn't want to question.

'How's Finn?' He almost pushed past her in his rush to get through the door.

She shook her head and stepped completely

aside. 'He's fine. He's just tired.' She pointed towards the sofa. She hesitated for a second. 'He had some dinner and he's sleeping now. But he was a little upset earlier.'

'He was? Is he sick?'

Riley turned towards her and she could instantly see his panic. She held up her hand in front of him. 'No, he's not sick. His pupils are equal and reactive. I gave him some kiddie paracetamol that I bought at the pharmacy. Yes, he felt a bit queasy for a while, but was fine after I'd fed him.' She took a deep breath. She was being automatically defensive because she wasn't that experienced with kids. Looking after kids with cystic fibrosis had been a whole different ball game. But she could imagine how Riley must have felt, thinking there was something wrong with Finn and he couldn't get there.

He crossed the room in a few strides and knelt down in front of the sofa. She watched as he gently stroked Finn's hair and whispered to him. 'Hey, buddy, sorry I was so long. I've missed you.'

The truth of every word that he said was etched

on his face, and she turned away as tears sprang to her eyes.

This guy was doing crazy things to her heart. His love. His connection to his child. That over-whelming parental urge that she'd never felt—and would never feel.

Or would she? When she'd seen Riley's name on the phone screen today her heart had been in her mouth. She'd been immediately worried about Finn. Seeing him, and knowing he was okay, had relieved her concerns instantly. Spend-ing time with him this afternoon had been a plea-sure—even though he'd been a little cranky.

His every move, every gesture had reminded her of Riley. Being with Finn today had made her realise that even though she'd made her decision about the future she still had the ability to love a child as if it were her own.

That had almost seemed like something so far out of her reach she hadn't even thought about it that much.

She'd been focused on making the decision and getting her surgery out of the way before she gave herself a chance to regroup and think about what the future might hold.

But the guy who was currently leaning forward, showing every element of being a doting dad, was wrapping her emotions up in knots and her interaction with Finn earlier had exposed her to some overwhelming feelings.

After a minute he came over and stood next to her. 'What happened?'

She sucked in a breath. All of a sudden she didn't really want to tell him. He was Finn's father. He had a right to know his child had been upset. But she couldn't quite extricate her own feelings from all of this. Not without revealing them to Riley.

She gave her head a shake. 'He misses his mum. He heard a woman outside call his name—her son must be called Finn too. For a few seconds I think he thought it was his mum and he got upset and was crying.'

Riley ran his fingers through his hair and shook his head. On top of the exhaustion that was already there, he almost looked broken. 'How do I deal with this, April? What do I do?'

She gulped at the pleading tone to his words. She wanted to wrap her hands around his neck and pull him close.

This was a conversation she couldn't have. She just couldn't.

Not the way she felt right now. He had no idea what she was preparing herself for. She turned and walked into the kitchen. She had to try to distance herself from this. She couldn't let Finn see her as some sort of mother figure. She couldn't let this potential relationship with Riley develop any further.

She kept her voice steady as she flicked on the kettle. 'You just be his dad, Riley. That's all you can do.'

She looked at the pained expression on his face and the sag of his shoulders. She'd never seen him look so tired. It was time to try to change the subject. 'What happened?' she asked.

He paused for a second and gave her a quizzical glance. She could almost see the words forming on his lips to ask her why she was pulling away, but in the end he gave a brief shake of his head. 'There was another RTA at another part of town. Turned out A&E also have a sickness bug. I had to travel with one of the patients in the ambulance. When I got there…' He let his voice trail off.

She nodded. 'You couldn't leave. You had to stay and help.'

He sighed. 'I'm a doctor; what else could I do? They didn't have enough staff to deal with two major RTAs. By the time I could hitch a lift back to the scene of the accident to pick up my car half the day had just gone. I'm sorry, April.'

She put her hand on his arm. 'It's fine. Really.'

He wrinkled his nose and squinted back at Finn. 'What is he wearing?'

April shrugged. 'He couldn't lie around in his school uniform. I gave him a T-shirt to wear. He picked it. It's a superhero one. He said it was better than the one with pink sequins.'

They'd laughed about it. Finn had been impressed with her variety of superhero T-shirts. He'd been even more impressed by her collection of superhero socks, especially when she'd whispered, 'I think these are mostly for boys. But girls need superheroes too. And I always have cold feet. So I need *lots* of socks.'

Riley smiled, shook his head and followed her into the kitchen. He looked around. 'Nice flat. Have you lived here long?'

She shook her head. 'Just since I took the job

at Waterloo Court.' She held up her hands in the glossy black kitchen. 'It was brand new when I bought it, and already finished, so I didn't have much say. Hence, the wooden floors throughout and the black kitchen.' She shrugged. 'I think they do up most new places the same these days. White walls, white bathrooms and very little personality.'

He pointed towards a large cardboard box tucked in the corner of the kitchen. 'What's that?'

She lifted a cup out of the cupboard. 'Oh, that's the Christmas tree. I just pulled it down from the loft last night. I have a little loft space because I'm the top floor flat. It's good. I'm secretly a hoarder, so I can hide all my junk up there.'

Riley stood up and lifted the edge of the cardboard box. His eyebrows shot up. 'A black Christmas tree? I thought you loved Christmas? This seems kinda weird.'

She smiled. 'Yeah, well. It fitted with the flat. It has purple baubles, though. I'm sure Finn will approve.' She wagged her finger. 'And, believe me, you have no idea just how many other Christmas decorations I actually have. Now, tea or coffee?' She held up both in her hands.

'What, no wine?'

She shook her head. 'Not on a school night. It seems like there's no dinner either. I bought something for Finn but forgot about myself. I can make you chicken nuggets if you want? Or cheese on toast.'

Riley let out a groan. 'Coffee, please. Just black since you don't have a fancy cappuccino maker. And I'd kill for some cheese on toast.'

She smiled as she opened the grill. 'I'm glad you appreciate my cooking talents.'

It only took a few minutes to start toasting the bread under the grill and to grate some cheese. Riley nursed his coffee as he watched.

'How was the accident? Was everyone okay?'

He sighed. 'Hopefully, yes. There was an elderly couple. The man has a broken tibia and fibula. He was pinned in the car and I waited until the fire brigade could cut him out. He was unconscious while I was there, but came around when he got transferred into the ambulance. The woman had a pneumothorax and a fractured tib and fib too. She needed a chest tube when she reached A&E and then had to go to emergency theatre. It took about three hours for the anaesthetist to agree to take her. The other two were a father and son. The little boy was unharmed and the father just had a head lac, and some burns from the airbag.'

'What happened?'

He shook his head. 'Apparently a deer ran across the road. Who knows where it came from.'

April turned around and bent down to watch the cheese on toast as it started to bubble. A few seconds later she slid the grill pan out and lifted the toast onto plates.

Riley was watching her carefully as she sat down opposite him. She could tell straight away that something was bothering him.

'Thank you,' he said. 'Thank you for picking up Finn and looking after him.' His bright green eyes were fixed on hers with an intensity she hadn't expected.

'No problem.' She looked at the cheese on toast. He hadn't started eating yet.

She could see his tongue pressed into the side of his cheek, as if he were contemplating saying something.

'What?'

SCARLET WILSON

He met her gaze with those green eyes. 'I didn't have anyone else to call.'

She shifted in her chair. 'So?'

He was still nursing the coffee cup in his hand. 'That's just it. I didn't have someone else to call for Finn.'

She wasn't quite sure where this was going but her skin prickled. 'But you called me, I picked him up, everything was fine.'

He shook his head. 'But it's not right. Finn should have more family than me. I should have more people around him.'

Her stomach started to churn. 'But you have your mum and dad. Didn't you say your mum wanted to move closer?'

He ran his fingers through his hair. She took a bite of her cheese on toast. She wasn't going to wait any longer.

'That's just it. I made a decision today.'

Uh-oh. This sounded serious. She swallowed quickly. 'What?'

He shook his head. 'I can't leave Finn. I just can't. Today, when I couldn't get to him, it made me re-evaluate everything. I'm going to speak to the Colonel. He's arranged things for me on a temporary basis. But I need to plan ahead.'

She gave a slow nod. 'You got a fright, Riley. That's understandable. It was unusual circumstances.' She gave him a smile. 'It's your first time in this situation as a dad. It will feel different.'

Riley was staring at his cheese on toast. It was as if it were easier to look at that than to look at April. 'Being a doctor, being in the army. It's all been about me. That has to stop. That has to change. I can't take an overseas posting again. Those days are gone. What happened if I was in Sierra Leone and Finn took ill? Who would take care of him?'

April had been about to take another bite and she froze, not quite sure where he was going next. Was he about to suggest her?

Please don't suggest me.

But Riley shook his head again. 'No. That's it. I'm done. I have to look for something else. Something that will suit Finn.'

She frowned, part of her brain so mixed up about this whole conversation. 'It doesn't matter what you do, Riley. There will always be days when you're not available. Maybe you just need to set up some kind of contingency plan?'

'Maybe I just need to have a look at my life and wonder how I got here.'

His tone had changed and she jerked her head up.

'What does that mean?'

'What kind of guy am I, that a girl I went out with for two months fell pregnant and didn't feel the urge to let me know? She didn't even seem to want my name on the birth certificate. No financial support. Nothing.'

These thoughts had already shot through her brain. But she shook her head. 'I can't speak for Isabel. I have no idea what she was thinking about. But she did leave a will. And she named you as the person to have Finn. If she thought so badly of you, she would never have done that.'

'Maybe she didn't have any other options? Isabel didn't have siblings, and her mum and dad were dead.' He said the words bitterly.

But April could think a bit clearer. 'No. She did have other options. One of her friends at the funeral said they'd offered to take Finn if something had happened. They'd had a drunken conversation once. But apparently Isabel said she'd made plans for Finn and she knew it was the right thing. She did have confidence in you, Riley. Even if you never had that conversation.'

There was silence for a few seconds. Then he kept going. 'April, how well do we know each other?'

He was jumping all over the place. She was going from confused to bewildered. 'Well…not very.' She hated saying that. It seemed odd. She'd been there when he'd found out about his child. She'd gone with him to his first meeting with his son. And now today, she'd been the person to cradle and hold Finn while he'd cried about his mother.

He set down the cup and drummed his fingers on the table. 'That's just it. How well did I know Isabel?'

She choked. 'Somehow I don't think it's the same thing.'

He gave the slightest shake of his head. 'But it is. What am I going to be able to tell Finn about his mum? I hear what you're saying but it still seems unreal. Why didn't she tell me about Finn? Did she think I was some kind of deadbeat? Some kind of unreliable guy that wouldn't pull his weight?'

She didn't even know how to start to answer that question. She shook her head gently. 'Maybe she was just an independent woman. Maybe getting pregnant was accidental; maybe it wasn't. Maybe she'd reached a stage in her life where she wanted to have a child and didn't want any complications.'

His gaze completely narrowed. He looked horrified. 'A complication? That's what I am? I'm his father!' His voice had risen in pitch and she shook her head and glanced through to Finn's sleeping form on the sofa.

'Shh. I know that. You're asking me to make guesses about someone I never even met. How can I do that? I have no idea what was going through Isabel's mind. How can I?' She took a deep breath. 'Somehow I don't think she'd write you off as a deadbeat. You're a doctor, Riley. It's hardly a deadbeat career. But maybe she thought if she told you that you might be angry with her. You said you were focused on your career. Maybe she knew that?'

He ran his fingers through his hair and closed

his eyes. 'But I've missed five years of my son's life. I've missed so much. I didn't hear his first word. I didn't see his first steps.' He shook his head again. 'I wasn't bad to Isabel. Why wouldn't she tell me?'

April ran her tongue along her lips. She could see his anguish. See how distraught he was about all this. The tiny fleeting thought she'd had a few months back entered her mind again. She'd considered going out and trying to get pregnant. It had been the briefest thought. A moment of madness. She could have done to some random stranger what Isabel had done to Riley.

'I have no idea about any of this, Riley. It's horrible. I know that. But this isn't about you. This is about Finn. You have to put all this aside. You can't let Finn know that you're angry at his mother. You can't let him see this resentment. Isabel obviously didn't need financial support from you.' She paused; something he'd said had just struck her. 'Your name—it isn't on Finn's birth certificate, is it?'

There was a real sadness, a weariness about him. 'No. I had a discussion with the social worker. The will was clear. That's why Finn is with me. But if I want to get my name on his birth certificate, there will need to be a DNA test and it will go through court. It's just a formality. But it will also help if I want to change Finn's name. Right now he's still Finn Porter. He should be Finn Callaghan.' He pushed the coffee cup away from him. 'This is such a mess, April. I want to do everything right. But I can't make up for five lost years. And the truth is I'm never going to get over that.'

She ached for him—she really did. Riley was a good man. The kind of man she'd spent part of her life searching for. But now that she'd found him?

It wasn't the right time. For either of them. And that made her sad. If she blinked she could imagine meeting him five years ago—when Isabel had. Before she'd known about her genetic heritage, before she'd lost her sister. When the world had still looked bright and shiny. Riley would have fitted in well.

If Finn was their child, would she have told him?

Of course she would have. She knew that with certainty.

But today she'd been overwhelmed by her motherly feelings towards Finn. They'd made her realise exactly what she was missing. Exactly what she would never be. And she wasn't ready for that. Not right now.

'You have to stop thinking about what you've lost, Riley.' She reached across the table and let her fingers brush against his. 'You have to start thinking about what you've gained. And that's the best little boy in the world.' She licked her lips again and prayed her voice wouldn't shake. Because she meant that—she truly did. 'Some people don't ever get that far. They never get that chance, no matter how much they want it. Count your blessings.'

He looked up sharply, his gaze melding with hers. She knew she'd revealed part of herself that she hadn't meant to. It was only words. And she hadn't actually told him anything. But Riley was a doctor. A good doctor. He would pick up on the words she wasn't saying.

He spoke carefully. 'You're right. Of course you're right. If someone had told me a few weeks ago how much my life could change...' His voice tailed off as he looked through at Finn.

Her heart swelled against her chest. A few weeks ago she would have said that Riley Callaghan was a cheeky charmer—a flirt, with good looks to match. It was part of the reason she'd kept her distance. She didn't want the pull; she didn't want the attraction. She had enough going on in her life.

But there was so much more to him. He was changing before her eyes. Watching him take these first few steps as a parent was enlightening. It was revealing more and more of the man to her. Was she really prepared for this?

'I need to sort things out. I need to make plans. Get things in place.' His voice cut through her thoughts.

She gave him a smile but his face was serious. 'And that starts with you, April.'

'What?' She sat forward in her chair.

He gestured towards her. 'You did me an enormous favour today. And there's always a chance I might ask it of you again. If that's okay with you, of course.'

She nodded automatically before she really had time to think about it. Her brain was screaming

No at her. But her heart had overruled her head in milliseconds.

Caution still niggled at her. Once she agreed a surgery date she'd be in hospital for a few days. She might not be able to drive for a few weeks after. She chose her words carefully. 'Do you really think that's a good idea? It's really important right now that you and Finn get a chance to bond. I think me being around could complicate matters.' She was trying to steal herself away in the easiest way possible.

Riley didn't seem to pick up on her cautionary words.

He held up his hands and looked around. 'I'm only asking you to be a second contact for Finn in case of emergency. Situations like today are unlikely to happen again. I just need a second number. You can do that, can't you? I think it's most important for Finn right now to be around people he can trust. Isn't it?'

She swallowed. When he said it out loud it made perfect sense. If she argued now it would make her look petty and small, and it might mean that Riley would ask more difficult questions.

She gave a brief nod. 'Okay, fine. You've got my number. You can use it.'

He smiled. 'Perfect, thank you.' Then he looked around. 'Since I'm trusting you with my son, I think we should get to know each other a little better. I've never been in here before. I only knew where you live because you came with me to pick up Finn. I feel as if I'm doing this all back to front.'

She shook her head. 'What are you talking about?'

'Okay. Tell me something about yourself. You picked up Finn today because you were the one person I could think of to phone—to trust with my child. But are we really even friends?'

Her stomach coiled. He was right. How well did they really know each other? What kind of movies did he like? What kind of food? Instinctively she felt as if Riley needed a giant bear hug. A simple show of affection because he'd had a bad day and was feeling so confused about things. That was the kind of thing you would do for a loved one—or for a friend.

But there was a prickliness to him. An edge. As if he just didn't know where he was in this life.

She recognised it because she'd worn it herself for so long.

It was almost like staring into a mirror and it made her heart flip over. Because, no matter how hard she tried to convince herself, she didn't think of Riley as a friend. It felt like so much more.

'I… I…think we're friends,' she said hesitantly, almost as if she were trying the word out for size. Why was that? Was it because saying she was Riley's 'friend' out loud didn't seem quite adequate?

He gave a nod. 'I would say so too. But we have gaps. We have bits missing.' He gave the tiniest wince. He already knew she hadn't talked about her sister much. Was he going to try to push her to talk more?

But he didn't. He just held up his hand towards her. 'Tell me something—' he paused '—not related to work. For example—' he frowned, as if trying to think of something himself '—tell me something most people wouldn't know about you. Like when I was a kid—' he put his hand on his chest and looked a bit sheepish '—I caused a panic on a beach once by saying I'd seen a shark.

Truth was, I didn't want to swim in the sea but didn't want my brother to know.'

Her mouth fell open. 'What?' She wrinkled her brow and leaned forward. 'Riley Callaghan, were you scared?'

He winked. 'My lips are sealed. I'll never tell. Now, your turn.'

She racked her brain for something equally odd. It was hard being put on the spot. After a few seconds something came to mind. 'Okay, I once tried to steal a chocolate bar from a shop. But I chickened out when my sister saw me.'

From the expression on his face that was the last thing he'd expected. He leaned forward. 'You? Really?'

Now she felt ridiculous. Where on earth had that come from?

She just nodded.

'Why?'

She threw up her hands. 'I don't know. I just wanted it, I suppose.'

Riley shook his head. 'What age were you?' He wasn't going to let this go.

'Five,' she snapped.

Now, he laughed. 'Okay, that was random…

and unexpected.' His hand crept towards the now cold cheese on toast. 'Tell me about your sister?'

Her skin prickled. 'What about her?'

'Let's start with her name.'

She wanted to change the subject. Her brain started thinking of random questions to throw at him.

Who was the first girl you slept with? was the one that danced around inside her head. But she didn't want to ask that. She didn't want to *know* that.

She imagined herself pulling on her big-girl pants.

'Mallory' was what she finally said.

He looked thoughtful. 'April and Mallory. Nice names, quite unusual.'

She nodded. 'My mother thought so. She picked April and my dad picked Mallory.'

'Ah, so they took turns? Interesting.'

She opened her mouth to say no. Then stopped. She hadn't told him Mallory was her twin. And she didn't want to. Not when she could guess where this conversation might lead.

'So you said that Mallory died eighteen months ago. I'm sorry. What happened?'

This was the second time he'd asked her. She tried not to let her voice shake, but she certainly couldn't meet his gaze. 'Mallory had cancer.'

'Oh. That's terrible. What kind?'

He hadn't missed a beat. She squeezed her eyes closed, just for a millisecond. He couldn't know the rest of what was going on in her head. He couldn't know the connections.

'Ovarian cancer,' she said quickly. 'She was unlucky.'

He pulled back a little. 'She was young.'

'Lots of people die young. It's a fact of life. Look at Isabel.'

It was a little bit cruel to turn it back around. But she needed to. She didn't want to have this conversation at all.

All it was doing was reinforcing the gulf that was between them. How far apart they really were.

The dreams of motherhood she'd felt earlier while looking at Finn? She had to push them away for now. Her stomach gave another twinge.

That was a few times that had happened now. What if it was...*something*?

It was as if the temperature had just plummeted

in her flat to freezing. One hand went automatically to her arm, rubbing up and down.

She was being ridiculous. It was nothing. Surgery was to be scheduled in the New Year. She always experienced painful periods. She often experienced ovulation pain too. It was just that. It must be.

Riley tilted his head and looked at her curiously—maybe even with a little disappointment. 'I guess you're right. It's still sad. For all parties.'

'I know.' It was a blunt response. But she just didn't want to go down this road.

He sucked in a deep breath. 'I'm going to be staying. I'm going to be staying at Waterloo Court for now and thinking about other options. We could be working together for a long time.'

His hands pressed together for a second on the table. Then he seemed to regain his focus. 'How do you feel about that?'

He wasn't looking at her. Her heart missed a beat, then started doing somersaults in her chest. Part of her was praying he wasn't about to suggest something more between them, part of her wishing that he would.

'What do you mean?' Her mouth seemed to go

into overdrive. 'That will be fine. You staying is what's best for Finn. It will give you a chance to get to know each other more.' She held up her hands casually. 'And work? That's just work.' She narrowed her gaze. 'We get on well at work, don't we?'

He looked a bit amused. 'I just wondered what you'd say.' He gave her a playful wink. 'Unless I'm buying you hot chocolate you seem to avoid me. Now that you're my emergency contact for Finn...' He let his voice tail off as he kept smiling at her. 'Thank you for saying yes. It means a lot. He knows you. He trusts you. *I* trust you.'

She blinked. It almost felt like diving off one of those high Greek cliffs over the perfect sea. That sensational plummet. There was nothing romantic about this. No promises or intentions. But there seemed to be a huge amount of unspoken words hanging in the air between them.

She'd thought he was attractive from the start. She'd deliberately tried to keep him at arm's length. And her instincts had been right, because being around Riley Callaghan was tougher than she had ever imagined.

Just being in his company made her wonder

about the brush of his skin next to hers. It sparked memories of the hug—that she'd initiated—and the reminder of what it was like to be close to someone.

She missed it. But it felt amplified around Riley. Because his company was so much more appealing than anyone else's.

And it was ridiculous, but an icy glove had just wrapped around her heart. After her feelings earlier around Finn it all seemed too much.

Her mouth was dry. She stood up, picking up her plate and cup. 'It's fine, providing I'm free and available.'

He smiled. 'Planning any month-long holidays in the near future?'

She shrugged. 'You never know. Things can come up.'

She kept her back to him and started washing up. The *I trust you* statement wasn't giving her the warm glow it probably should. And this wasn't about Finn. None of this was about Finn.

This was about her and how mixed up she was about everything.

This was about the fact that for the first time in a long time she'd started to feel attraction and a pull towards another human being. And it wasn't just that it didn't fit in with her plans.

This was all about Finn. Just like it should be. The only reason Riley was staying in one place now was because of the unexpected arrival of Finn.

He wouldn't have stayed here for her. No, he would have been on that plane to Sierra Leone, probably with a sigh of relief and a smile on his face. Riley Callaghan would just have been a doctor she'd briefly worked with at some point.

But was that really what she wanted?

Riley appeared at her side with his cup and plate. It seemed he'd managed to eat the cold cheese on toast after all. 'I'll take Finn home now,' he said quickly. 'Thanks for looking after him. I appreciate it. How about I pick you up on Saturday and you can help us pick a Christmas tree? I think it would be good for him. He's already said he wants you to come with us.' He let out a short laugh and looked at her cardboard box. 'Maybe you want to trade yours in? Or buy some new decorations for your hidden stash?'

He had no idea. No idea of the crazy thoughts that had just pinged about her head and her heart.

She moved into self-protection mode. She could do this. She could make completely inane conversation. She could find a way to make a suitable excuse.

'Oh, I'm not sure. I was going to do some Christmas shopping. Try and get a head start on things.'

Riley had already walked through to the main room. 'Well, that's perfect. You love Christmas. I love Christmas,' he said easily. 'You can do your shopping at the garden centre.'

For a second she was stunned. She hadn't quite been ready for that one.

He pulled his jacket over Finn, picked him up and walked over to the front door. 'See you later,' he said as he opened the door and walked out into the foyer.

April was a bit stunned. Her plan was to say no. Her plan was to create some distance between herself and Riley.

She closed her door and sagged against it.

She was becoming more confused by the second.

He'd almost said something. He'd almost hinted to her that maybe they should reconsider their relationship. What relationship? He wasn't even capable of having a relationship. At least, that was what Isabel must have assumed since she hadn't even told him about his son. He was still struggling with that.

It was just, for a few minutes today, he'd looked at April sitting across the table from him and been overwhelmed by the sadness in her eyes. That was why he'd pressed her. That was why he'd been quite pointed.

He liked her. He more than liked her. If he was being truthful, he might actually care. She was a good person. She was the only person he'd considered when he'd realised he couldn't get to Finn.

But even before Finn, even before he'd realised the enormity of being a dad, there had still been something about April. He could remember, as clear as day, that overwhelming lift he'd felt when she'd appeared in the pub and he'd thought, for just a second, she might actually have come to see him.

And she had. Just not in the way he had hoped for.

When he watched her with Finn it was like a little clenched-up part of him just started to unfurl.

He knew he should only concentrate on his son. Finn had lost the person that he knew best. Riley was playing rapid catch-up. And sometimes feeling like a poor replacement.

But April was constantly around the edges of his thoughts. And she had a shell of her own. He knew that. He could tell. She was doing her best to keep him at arm's length.

It was almost as if they were doing a dance around each other. He liked her. She liked him. Sometimes when their gazes connected he could see the sparks fly. Other times he could almost see her retreat into herself.

And she'd hinted at something today. As if she might be going somewhere in the future. At least that was what he thought. Was she considering another job? Would that mean she wouldn't be around?

That thought sent a wave of cool air over his skin.

He just didn't know what to do next.

The more time he spent with April Henderson, the more time he *wanted* to spend with her. She was infectious. And being in her company made him happy. Made Finn happy. He wanted to act on the pull between them—but did she?

He already knew he wouldn't sleep tonight. He'd be too busy watching over his son. It didn't matter that, as a doctor, he would say it wasn't necessary. Right now he wasn't a doctor; he was a parent.

He also knew that April was going to haunt his thoughts tonight.

He'd watched her try to make an excuse for Saturday but he'd already decided he wouldn't listen.

Chipping away at April Henderson's armour was helping him chip away at his own. He just wasn't quite sure where it would lead.

CHAPTER SEVEN

EVEN THOUGH IT was early afternoon, the sky was already darkening and the lights from the garden centre twinkled in greeting to them. Finn pressed his nose up against the window of the car, sending steamy breaths up that smoked his view. 'Is this where we get the Christmas tree?'

April nodded. She'd spent the last few days trying to make up an excuse not to be around Finn and Riley—each of them more pathetic than the one before. Her stomach had been in a permanent knot for the last few days. Finally, she'd realised it was almost like being a teenager going on a first date. Mallory used to tease her relentlessly about it. April had nearly always been sick before a first date, whereas Mallory had walked about the house singing.

And as soon as she'd had that thought, she knew she was going to go.

She smiled at Finn. 'They have lots to choose from. You'll find the perfect one.'

Riley opened the door of the car for Finn so he could climb out. The car park was busy; a group of children were crowded around the outside display—Santa's sleigh being pulled by reindeers.

'Look!' gasped Finn as he wriggled free of Riley's grasp and ran over to lean on the barrier. He stretched to touch the carved wooden reindeers. The largest one was just out of his reach. April looked around and gave him a bump up, so his fingertips could brush against the roughened wood. 'I touched him!' Finn squealed excitedly. 'I touched Rudolph!' April laughed as she let him down. Sure enough, someone in the garden centre had painted the nose of this reindeer bright red. Finn pulled her down towards him and whispered in her ear, his eyes sparkling, 'Are these the real reindeers? Do they come to life on Christmas Eve so they can deliver all the presents?'

April glanced conspiratorially around her. 'What do you think?' she whispered back. Finn's smile spread from ear to ear. Riley was standing behind them with his hands in his pockets.

'Come on, you guys. Let's go pick a tree.'

April nodded; she slipped her hand into Finn's and he took it without question. As they walked through the main entrance she gestured to a blacked-out area to the left. 'All the neon trees are in here. The real trees are on the other side. I wasn't quite sure what you would want.'

Riley bent down to Finn. 'Should we take a look at them all?'

Finn nodded excitedly. The area was encased by a giant black tent and, as soon as they pushed the curtain aside, Finn gasped. The tent was full of trees, all different sizes, all pre-lit, some multi-coloured, others with just white lights. Some of the lights were programmed, twinkling intermittently, or staying bright the whole time. Finn walked slowly from one tree to the other, stopping in front of one tree that was covered in bright blue lights. 'I like this one, Dad,' he breathed.

Riley glanced at April, then bent forward and lifted the price tag. His face gave a twisted look. He turned the tag towards her and mouthed, 'How much?'

She laughed. 'Come on, Finn.' She gave his

hand a tug. 'Let's look at them all before we make a decision.'

They walked out of the tent, past all the rope lights for decorating the front of houses, and an array of illuminated parcels, Santas and white reindeers. The back of the tent led out into the middle of the garden centre, with tinsel and tree decorations as far as the eye could see.

Riley blinked. He turned and put his hand on April's waist. 'Boy, Christmas is really a big production, isn't it?'

'And you want to buy a house?' she quipped. 'By the time we leave here, you won't be able to afford a house.'

The decorations were all organised by colour. Finn made his way over to the red ones, his little fingers touching everything that was hanging on the wall in front of him. April laughed at Riley flinching every time Finn stretched for something delicate-looking. 'Let him look,' she said quietly. 'It's part of the fun.'

Riley rolled his eyes. 'I can see me leaving here with an enormous bill and not a single thing to show for it.'

She shook her head. 'Don't worry; they're used to children.'

They spent nearly an hour, Finn running between the coloured displays then back into the tented area. Finally, April pointed to outside. 'Do you want to go and see the real Christmas trees?'

Finn nodded and slipped his hand into hers. Her heart swelled. It was ridiculous—it didn't mean anything. But the warmth of that little hand in hers sent a whole wave of emotions circling around her body.

Riley held the door and they headed outside. In the space of an hour, the last elements of light had gone, leaving the perfect backdrop for viewing the real Christmas trees, which were planted in lines and all currently topped with a dusting of snow.

April sucked in a breath. 'Well, this is definitely the place to pick a Christmas tree.'

Riley brushed against her. 'I think you could be right.'

Finn's hand slipped from hers and he ran yelling down the middle of the path. 'This is great!' he shouted, holding out his hands to brush against the trees.

'Eek!' April took off after him and swept her arms around him. 'Watch out—you might damage some of the trees. And you've not picked your own yet.'

He looked a little disappointed, his head turning from side to side. 'But how do you pick a tree?' He wrinkled his nose. 'What's the strange smell?'

Riley laughed. 'It's all the trees. Haven't you had a real one before?'

Finn shook his head, so Riley knelt down in front of him. 'Well, now is the time to decide. Do you want a light-up tree from inside, or a real one from outside?'

Finn looked confused. 'Does the real one go in the garden, or go in the house?'

'It goes in the house.'

He touched the nearest tree. 'But if we pick one of these does that mean our Christmas tree has no lights?'

Riley shook his head. 'We just buy some lights separately. We need to buy some Christmas baubles too.'

Finn looked thoughtful. He started to walk in amongst the row of trees again. April and Riley exchanged glances and followed him around. There were plenty of other families at the garden centre picking Christmas trees. April realised that people would assume the same about them—that they were a family. Her heart gave a squeeze as she realised how much she'd wished for something like this.

Riley was confusing. It was clear he was trying his best with Finn. It was clear he was learning along the way. And so was she.

She couldn't work out in her head how she felt about all this. She'd been attracted to Riley from the start, but he was only there for a short time and she hadn't been in a place to begin a relationship.

Now, he was staying. And she wasn't entirely sure how happy he was about it. It was clear he loved his son. But his career plans had just been halted abruptly.

And the constant lingering looks made her wonder what else there could be between them. Riley was flirtatious. He hadn't mentioned any significant long-term relationships in the past. Who knew what he'd want in the future?

She hadn't even revealed her health issues to

him. It was quite likely that Riley might see his future with more children in it. That couldn't happen with her.

She had surgery to go through. There would always be that threat of cancer somewhere in the background.

That could be true for a lot of people. She was well aware that one in three adults in the UK would develop cancer at some point in their lives. But, even with surgery, chances were her odds would be higher.

The long and short of it was that she was a risk.

Finn had already lost a parent. Was it fair she might even consider being a part of his life— even as a friend?

As for Riley… She squeezed her eyes closed for a second. Finn was running around a Christmas tree now. He seemed to have picked his favourite. And Riley was joining in and chasing him around.

Her heart ached. She liked this man far more than she should. He was a charmer. Last thing he needed in his life was a woman with a potential ticking cancer and no ability to have children.

There was a real pang deep inside as she

watched Finn. Another woman was standing to her side with a small curly-haired girl, and her stomach swollen. April turned away quickly. She didn't want to get emotional. Since she'd made her decision about the surgery it seemed as if the world was full of pregnant women.

It felt as if the number of female staff she worked with who'd announced they were pregnant recently had doubled. It could be that there was something in the air. Or it could be that she was noticing more, and becoming more sensitive to it.

She gritted her teeth. Her decision would give her a better chance at *life*. A life she should embrace. A life she would live on behalf of herself, and her sister.

'Okay?' Riley came up behind her, his breath visible in the cold air, his cheeks tinged red and his eyes shining. He caught the expression on her face. 'What's wrong?'

She shook her head. 'Nothing. Nothing at all. Are you done?'

He gestured with his hand towards the tree Finn was still dancing around. 'We've picked our tree.

I've spoken to the sales guy. They'll deliver it. We just need to pick some decorations.'

For a second she thought she might have to paste a smile on her face. But she didn't. The warm feeling of being around Riley and Finn was spreading through her stomach and up towards other parts.

'Great. Let's get back inside.' She rubbed her hands together.

Riley looked down and closed his hands over hers, rubbing them with his own. 'Are you cold? Sorry, I didn't think.'

The gentle heat from his hands was so personal. So unexpected. He smiled as he did it for a few seconds. 'I should buy you some gloves.' He pulled his hands away and turned back to Finn. 'Come on, Finn. April's getting cold. Come and pick some lights.'

Finn turned at his father's shout and ran straight to them. 'What colour? What colour will we get?'

Riley slid his hand around Finn's shoulders. 'Well, you get to pick. I don't have any decorations yet, so you can pick your favourite.'

She followed them back into the darkened area. The lights twinkled all around them. It wasn't just lights. There was a whole array of illuminated animals at their feet, and a whole Christmas village on a table too. April wandered over. She knew as soon as Riley was at her back as she could smell his woody aftershave. 'What are you looking at?' he whispered.

She bent down to get a closer look. 'This village. I just love it. Look, there's a schoolroom. A bakery. Santa's workshop. A church. A shop. There's even a skating rink.'

Riley was right behind her and, instead of stepping around her, he just slid his hand forward, brushing against her hip as he turned one of the price tags over. His cheek was almost touching hers. 'They're not too expensive.' Then he gave a low laugh. 'That's if you only buy one. If you buy the whole village…'

She laughed too, leaning back a little, her body coming into direct contact with his. Neither moved. It was as if both of them just paused, and sucked in a breath.

After the longest time Riley spoke, his warm breath at her neck. 'Which is your favourite?'

She looked over the village again. There were tiny characters in every scene, packages on shelves, mounds of snow at doorways, each one gently lit. Everything was so detailed. She sighed. 'I don't know. I think I love them all. I want the whole village.'

She reached down and picked up the toyshop. 'This is like the kind of thing where you could buy one every year, build up your collection and keep them for ever.'

He was smiling at her, only inches from her face. He reached and brushed a strand of hair away from her eyes, his hand covering hers as she held the shop. 'So how about you let me buy you your first one? As a thank you,' he added, 'for coming here with us today.'

The twinkling lights were behind them, but even though his face was in shadow his green eyes seemed brighter than ever. And they were focused totally on her.

She held her breath. Her hand itched to reach up and touch his dark hair that glistened with moisture from the snow outside. His cheeks were tinged with pink. Those green eyes were still, just locked with hers, and as she watched he licked his lips. Every nerve in her body was on fire. Every sense on overload.

He reached up again, this time his finger touching her cheek. 'Let me do something for you, April.'

The rush of emotion tumbled through her in waves. When was the last time someone had spoken to her like that? When was the last time she'd wanted someone to get this close? It felt like for ever. It felt like a whole lifetime ago.

A lifetime before her sister's vague symptoms. Shock diagnosis. Frantic treatment attempts. And the life just slowly draining from her body.

He made the smallest move. His cheek touched hers as his lips brushed against her ear. 'A toyshop. Along with the superhero T-shirts, I think you might secretly be a *Peter Pan* kind of girl.'

She could sense he was smiling.

Her eyes were closed, the toyshop held in front of her chest. She turned towards him just as his head pulled back from her ear.

Every part of her literally ached. Ached for his lips to touch hers.

Then, before she had time to think any more, his lips brushed against hers. The sensation was just as sweet as she'd imagined. Every bit as magical.

His hand tangled in her hair as the gentlest pressure increased.

She wanted this. She wanted this more than she'd ever imagined.

But just this—the slightest kiss—put her sensations into overload. Every part of her brain fired. She was starting something she might not be able to continue. She was taking what could not be hers. She was kissing a man she hadn't been entirely truthful with.

She trembled as the feelings threatened to overwhelm her and her eyes filled with tears. She pulled back.

Riley rested his head against hers. 'April? What's wrong? Did I do something wrong?'

She shook her head quickly. 'No. Of course you didn't.'

'But—' he started.

She placed her hand on his chest and gave him a regretful smile. Everything about the kiss had been right.

And everything about the kiss had been wrong.

'It's just not the right time,' she said as she looked around.

For a brief second she could see the flash of

confusion, but then he glanced around and gave a nod.

Her heart squeezed in her chest. He thought she meant here, in the garden centre, was the wrong time. But she meant so much more than that.

Riley looked around and spotted Finn racing around a Christmas tree. He gave an approving smile and dropped to his knees, looking under the table and emerging with a box in his hand. 'Look. The toyshop. You can take it home.'

She felt a pang inside.

Home. She wasn't quite sure what that meant for her any more.

Her flat had seemed so empty the other night after Finn and Riley had left. Her footsteps had echoed around the place. She'd never noticed that before.

Before it had been her haven. Her quiet place. Now, she was just conscious of the fact it had seemed so full with the two of them in it.

'Dad! I want these ones!' Both of them jerked at the sound of Finn's voice. He'd found blue twinkling stars wrapped around one of the trees.

Riley nodded in approval. He gave her a wink. 'Come on then. We've got more shopping to do.'

He walked off towards Finn and her stomach clenched. Riley had the box with the toyshop tucked under his arm. He was going to buy it for her.

As a thank you.

But when she'd thought about buying a piece of the village every year, she'd never really imagined just doing it for herself. She'd imagined it with a family around her.

Finn squealed as his dad threw him up in the air. 'April, I've picked the blue ones! Come and see.'

Her lips tingled. Riley's aftershave still filled her senses.

She glanced around. Christmas surrounded her. Both the best and worst time of year for some people. She could almost hear Mallory's voice in her head urging her on.

One kiss. That was all it had been. But she wanted so much more.

Right now, it just didn't feel honest, and she hated that more than anything. She licked her lips and looked around.

Was it wrong to want to enjoy this time with Riley and Finn? Was it wrong to join in with their celebrations? Mallory was whispering in her ear again. *Go on.*

Riley caught her eye. 'Okay?' he mouthed.

She nodded and walked over to join them. It was time to stop brooding about things and start enjoying life. 'Come on, guys.' She looked at the toyshop box and the Christmas lights. 'Oh, no, we're not finished yet. Someone grab a basket. We're going to shop till we drop.'

CHAPTER EIGHT

PLANS SEEMED TO be bursting from his head. Riley was buzzing. He couldn't wait to find April and tell her.

For the first time since all this had happened, things seemed to be falling into place.

He'd kissed her. He'd finally kissed her and it just felt so right. And all he could think about was kissing her again.

Okay, so she'd pulled back. Maybe April was more private than most. Maybe she didn't like being kissed in a public place. But that was okay. He could handle that. He could deal with that.

As long as he could kiss her again.

And even though he was currently bursting with excitement there was a tiny part of him that wondered if there could be something else— something else going on with April. He was sure it wasn't another man. April would never have let their spark and attraction grow if there was another man in the background.

She still hadn't really talked that much about her sister. Maybe it was just Christmas and the time of year? It just felt as if there was something he couldn't quite put his finger on yet. But he had to give her space. If he wanted to have some kind of relationship with April, he had to trust her to tell him the things he needed to know. Right now he should be concentrating on Finn.

His mother had stopped calling ten times a day. April had shown him a Top Ten list of Christmas toys for boys and it had been the biggest blessing in disguise. Finn seemed to like a whole range of things, so he'd handed the list over to his mother and asked her to track down what she could.

She'd been delighted. It had been a brilliant idea and he could hug April for it. Gran was over the moon to have a task related to her grandson and was tackling the list like a seasoned pro.

Finn seemed to be settling well. The crying at night had stopped after the first week. He was still wistful at times, and Riley encouraged him to talk about his mum as often as he liked.

Riley was finally making peace with the pictures of Isabel around the place. April had been right. It was good for Finn and that was what mattered. And, if all went to plan, they would have a place to permanently call home soon.

Work was still something he had to sort out, but he had plans for that too.

But he still didn't really have plans in his head for April.

He liked her. He more than liked her. He wanted to move things on. As soon as he set foot on the ward in the morning, the first thing he did was look for the swing of her blonde ponytail. Last night he'd nearly texted her around five or six times. He'd had to dial back in and only text twice. And it was all nonsense. Nothing that couldn't wait until the next time he saw her. But that had just seemed too far away.

If the phone buzzed and the screen lit up with her name he could feel the smile on his face before he'd even pressed the phone to his ear.

And it was ridiculous. Because sometimes it was actually about work.

He knew he should only be concentrating on Finn. Of course he should be. But there was something about April Henderson. The way she sometimes caught his gaze and gave him a quiet smile. The expression on her face when they'd been in the garden centre and she'd looked at all the Christmas decorations. But, more importantly, it was how he *felt* around her. It had been a long time since his heart had skipped a few beats at the sight of a woman. It had been a long time since he'd met someone he'd felt a real connection to. But even though it had been the briefest kiss, even though they hadn't really acted yet on the growing bond between them, Riley knew that at some stage he would take things further.

He knew there was more. Her sister had died of ovarian cancer. That must have been tough. It must have been a shock for her family. Maybe she was just quiet right now because it was the lead-up to Christmas. Tomorrow would be the first day of December. Finn would get to open the first door on his Advent calendar, though Riley was almost sure it wouldn't last that long.

In the meantime, Riley had to find April. He wanted to share his news. Maybe when she knew for sure that he and Finn planned on staying around it might take them to the next stage.

He'd told her he was staying, but she'd looked as if she hadn't really been convinced.

His plans had changed. He'd found what he had been looking for, but the funny thing was, when he'd seen the house he hadn't just imagined Finn and himself being in it. If someone had told him this a few months ago, that he could see himself staying in one place and settling down, he wouldn't have believed them. But April was making those plans seem real. They weren't even dating yet. But he planned on remedying that soon.

Maybe proving he planned on staying around could be the key to opening her heart.

'Come here—I want to show you something.'

April looked over her shoulder. No one else was around. 'Are you talking to me?' She couldn't stop the little pang she felt as soon as she heard his voice.

Riley glanced around. 'Who else would I be talking to? Here—' he spun the laptop around '—look at this.'

She bent down to see what he'd pulled up. Her eyebrows shot up. 'A house?'

He nodded. The excitement was written all over his face as his fingers moved over the keyboard.

She wasn't quite sure what to say. 'But Finn has just moved here. You can't want to move him again?' She'd phrased it as a question, but she hoped he'd get the hint.

He looked at her in surprise. 'But where we're staying is only temporary. It won't do. Not long-term.'

She licked her lips. 'So…your long-term is here?'

He shrugged. 'I told you it was. Where else would it be?'

This was going to take longer than she'd thought. She hitched her hip up onto the desk. 'Have you spoken to the Colonel?'

He shook his head. 'But I did try and get an appointment. Why?'

She wasn't part of the forces but had been here long enough to know how things usually worked. 'I thought he just let you stay here as a temporary measure? Won't you maybe have to change regiment or posting to get a permanent head-quarters?'

What she really wanted to say was, *Are you crazy for considering buying a house right now?*

But she didn't. She kept her thoughts in her head. Riley flicked through the pictures. It was a large grey Georgian sandstone semi. The house was full of character. Original doors, large sash windows with internal shutters. A huge fireplace. A large drawing room, separate dining room and a smaller room at the back they could make into a snug. A kitchen that had been renovated with a Belfast sink. Two bathrooms. The wide entrance-way and sweeping staircase gave her a pang of envy. Long-term, she'd always wanted to own a house like this. The bedrooms. Three of them. And a large garden at the back of the house—big enough for a kid to play football in.

Riley couldn't stop smiling and she wasn't quite sure what to say. It was ideal—a family home and something like that seemed so far out of her grasp right now.

She could almost picture the perfect woman who'd be standing next to him in a few years with a new baby in a pram to complete the family. And that hurt in a way she could never have imagined.

'It's for sale, but I could temporarily rent it for a few months—try it out for size—with a view to buying it. It's even in the right catchment area for Finn's school.' He gave her a nudge with his elbow. 'See? I'm learning.'

He was. Riley was getting the hang of things quicker than she'd given him credit for. He had no idea about the fact she could barely breathe right now.

Since when had she started having such irrational thoughts?

'When could you start renting?' she managed to ask.

'This week,' he answered quickly. 'The owner has moved to Japan. He just really wants someone to either buy the house or move in and take care of it.'

April thudded backwards in her seat. She still wasn't sure what to say. Riley hadn't seemed to notice. He was either too excited or too swept up in the idea to figure out she'd stopped talking.

He sat back too. 'So, if I sign the agreement tomorrow, Finn and I can move in the next few days.' He pointed at some of the décor. 'It maybe isn't perfect but it's in good condition. I can give the place a lick of paint. That's all it really needs.'

The thoughts jumbling around in April's mind started to sort themselves into some kind of order. Practical things. That was what she could think of. At least they were the kind of things she could say out loud. 'You'll need furniture. You don't have a sofa or a dining room table. Or beds. It's only a few weeks until Christmas. Riley, do you have any idea how much stuff you'll need?' She started to shake her head.

The smile had faded a little. 'Well, just the stuff you've said. A sofa, a table and some beds. What else is there?'

April leaned forward and pulled a piece of paper from the printer. 'Here, let me get you started.' She wrote down the things they'd just mentioned, then started adding more. 'Cushions, cutlery, dishes, lamps, towels, bedding…' She frowned and turned the computer towards her. 'What comes with the kitchen? Do you need a washer, dryer and fridge freezer?'

Riley looked pale. 'You're beginning to sound like my mother.'

'Does your mother think you need a reality

check?' She sighed and put down the pen. 'What happens if they move your base?'

He pressed his lips together and looked around. 'I might not be in the army much longer.'

'What?' She couldn't help it—she said the word much louder than she meant to.

'Shh—' he put his finger to his lips '—I haven't decided yet. I've just started to look into other options.'

'Like what?' A strange feeling was spreading through her. Like any serviceman, there was always a chance he would get moved. But she hadn't expected him to consider other options like this.

'I've looked at a few things. I could go into one of the training schemes at the local general hospital. I have a lot of experience. The most natural places would be accident and emergency, general surgery or orthopaedics.' He held up his hands. 'I could even look into infectious diseases, but the nearest place for that is around thirty miles away. Or...' His voice tailed off.

'Or what?' She was incredulous. When had he had a chance to think about any of this—his career plans or the house?

'I could think about training as a GP. It takes a year, and would have better hours for me.'

'You could still work here.' Where had that come from? And even she could hear the edge of desperation in her voice. 'Not all the staff here are service personnel. There's a mix of NHS and army personnel throughout Waterloo Court.'

He met her gaze. It was the first time since they'd sat down. 'I don't know if rehab is for me, April.'

It was like a spear into her heart. She gulped. He wasn't talking directly about her, but he might as well have. This was the place she'd chosen to work. This was the career path she wanted. It didn't matter that only a few weeks ago she'd known in her heart that he wasn't really a rehab doctor. It was all right for her to think those things. It felt entirely different when *he* said them to her.

It was almost as if Riley was saying it wasn't good enough for him.

She stood up, letting the chair roll away behind her. 'Well, I guess that's all up to you, isn't it? I have patients to see in the other ward. Good luck.'

She stalked off, picking up her blue coat and

shoving her arms into it, all the while trying to figure out why she really just wanted to cry.

Riley stared at April's retreating back. He wasn't quite sure what he'd just done.

He was only being honest. What was so wrong with that?

But part of him was uncomfortable. He hadn't meant to say anything that offended. But he was disappointed. He'd thought she'd be excited for him. Thought she might suggest talking over career plans with him. Maybe even suggest dinner. Instead she'd acted as if he'd just said he had the most infectious disease on the planet and made a run for it.

He shook his head. Since when had he got so bad at all the woman stuff?

Riley had never had problems getting dates. Never had problems with dating for a few months at a time. He might have had the odd few issues when he'd broken things off. But that had all been about his career. He didn't want long-term when he knew he was going to be away for months at a time.

He hadn't even got to the date stage with April.

Though there was no denying that was where he'd like to go.

In fact, he'd like to go a whole lot further.

He sighed, leaned back and put his hands behind his head.

What was he doing?

Was he crazy? She was gorgeous. She was fun when she wanted to be. She was sexy. She was sweet. She was great with Finn. But, most importantly, he'd found himself gravitating towards her more and more. He wasn't imagining things. There was a definite tug between them. April Henderson had well and truly buried her way under his skin.

And up until a few seconds ago that had made him happy.

For too long he'd focused his life on his job. Training as a doctor had taken all his energy; serving in the army had helped him focus. Moving around every six months had meant he was constantly meeting new faces and always learning to adapt. The medical situations were frequently frantic. Setting up in emergency situations was exhausting, and the long hours were draining. But for a long time Riley had thrived in that environment. He'd frequently been praised for his clinical care and cool head in a storm.

Thinking about a new career path was daunting. But since finding out about Finn he was just so anxious to get things right.

April pushed the door open, letting an icy blast sweep past him as she vanished out into the snow, and his heart gave a little tug. He liked her. He *more* than liked her. And that was so different from being attracted to her. At least it was in his head. Because that was the way he'd lived his life for the last twelve years.

So many things were changing. Was he changing too?

Finn flashed into his head. His laugh, his smile, the way he said the word *Dad*. All his energy right now should be focused on the little boy who needed him most. He didn't have room for anything else. But when he closed his eyes for a second Finn's face was replaced by the hurt expression on April's.

In an ideal world he would have liked it if she'd told him she loved the house and thought it was perfect. His stomach coiled. Perfect for whom?

'Stuff it!' he said out loud as he grabbed his jacket from the chair beside him.

The snow had picked up as he ran outside. The other ward was based on the other side of the courtyard, but right now he couldn't even see that.

He stopped. April hadn't made it to the other ward. She was standing in the middle of the court-yard, snow falling all around her. His footsteps slowed as he pulled on his jacket and walked over to her.

It was bitter cold. The snow was falling in thick flakes all around them. April had her hands at her throat, fingering her necklace, with hot, angry tears spilling down her face.

He cringed. No. He'd made her cry. And he didn't even really understand why.

'April? What's wrong? What is it?' He put his hands on her upper arms.

She tried to shake him off but he stayed firm. She shook her head. 'Nothing. Everything. I don't know!'

Her hair had loosened from her bobble and was straggling around her face. She looked so hurt. So desperate. This couldn't just be about him.

He took in a deep breath of the icy air. 'Talk to me, April. I'm right here. Just talk to me.'

She was shaking. She was actually shaking. He looked from side to side. 'Let's get inside. Let's get somewhere warm.'

She shook her head again. 'No. I don't want to. I need air. I need fresh air. I need to think straight.'

'What do you need to think about, April?'

This was killing him. He could see how upset she was, how much pain she was in. But he couldn't understand it.

'The house,' she breathed.

'You don't like the house?' He was confused.

Tears were still spilling down her cheeks. 'I love it.'

Now it was Riley who shook his head. 'April, you have to help me out here. I don't understand what's wrong. I don't understand what you're so upset about.' His insides were churning.

His grip tightened on her arms. 'Why won't you talk to me? Why do you keep pushing me away?'

Her face crumpled and he couldn't stop the stream of thoughts in his head. 'Is it me? Is it Finn? Don't you like being around kids?'

She shook her head.

Exasperation was building.

'April, you're gorgeous. And even though you try to pretend you're not, you're a people person. Why don't you have a husband? Why isn't there a boyfriend? I bet you could have a string of dates if you wanted.' Now he'd started he couldn't stop. 'And don't tell me you're not interested.' He moved over to her so he was only inches from her face. 'I see it, April. I sense it. We don't need electricity for Christmas lights. There's enough between us to light up the whole house—a whole street. What's happened to you, April? What's happened that you won't let anyone get close to you? What's happened that you won't let *me* get close to you?'

She shook her head. He could sense her frustration. It almost equalled his. But she just seemed so determined to keep him shut out. 'Don't ask. Just don't. I don't want to talk about it.' The blue of her coat seemed to make her eyes even brighter. It didn't matter how cold it was out here, or how cold she pretended her heart was, he wouldn't move away from her. He couldn't move away from her. He'd never felt so connected to—and yet so far away from—someone.

He couldn't hide the wave of concern that swept over him, feeling instantly protective towards her. 'Are you hurt? Has someone done something to you?'

He reached up and touched her cheek. 'April? Tell me—I want to help you.'

She blinked. Several heavy snowflakes had landed on her eyelashes. Those blue eyes fixed on his. He'd never seen anyone look so beautiful. So vulnerable. So exquisite.

The urge that had been simmering beneath the surface since the first time he'd seen her, the one that had spent the last few weeks threatening to bubble over at any point, just couldn't stay hidden any more. Riley had always been an action kind of guy.

She wouldn't speak to him. She wouldn't tell him what was wrong and that meant he didn't know how to support her—what to say to make things better.

But sometimes actions spoke louder than words.

'April,' he whispered, 'please tell me you don't

have a husband, fiancé or boyfriend hidden away somewhere.'

Her eyes widened. She shook her head. 'No. Why?'

'Because I have to do this again. I have to show you how I feel about you.'

He bent his head and kissed her. Her lips were cold. Her cheeks were cold. But it only took a few seconds to heat them up. April tasted exactly the way he remembered. Sweet. Pure. Exciting. Like a world of possibilities. And the perfect fit for him.

At first she didn't move. Then her lips gradually opened, her head tilting to allow their mouths to meld against each other.

He couldn't remember ever feeling a kiss like this. The tingles. The flip flops in his stomach. His hand slid from her soft cheek, tangling through her messy hair and anchoring at the back of her head. Her hands moved too. Sliding up around his neck. Her body moved closer to his.

It didn't matter that they were both covered by thick jackets. He could still feel her curves against his, sense the tilt of her hips towards him as her light floral scent drifted up around them.

In a way, being out in the snow was the perfect place for this kiss. They both loved Christmas. And there was nothing more Christmassy than snow.

Their kiss was deepening. It was almost as if he couldn't get close enough to her. To get enough of April Henderson. His brain was going to a million different places right now. Of course he wanted to know what was really going on with April. But kissing her had just seemed like the right thing to do.

The only thing that made sense to him. Her cold nose touched his cheek and he laughed, their lips finally parting. But he didn't want to part. And it seemed neither did she.

They stood for a few seconds with their foreheads pressing together as the snow continued to fall all around them. Their warm breath instantly steamed in the freezing air.

Riley couldn't help but smile. 'Should I apologise for kissing you?'

'Don't you dare' was the prompt reply, but after a second she gave a little shudder.

'What's wrong? Are you cold?'

She pulled back a little. 'I'm sorry, Riley. I can't do this.'

She was saying the words, but he could see the look in her eyes. It was almost as if she felt she *had* to say it, instead of wanting to say it.

'Why, April? Why can't you do this? This is the second time I've kissed you and the second time you've pulled back.'

She bit her lip. She lifted her hand to her necklace again. What was it about that charm?

'Is this about Finn?' Guilt started to swamp him. He was just coming to terms with being a father. His head was telling him he had to concentrate all his time and energy on that. And he would. Finn needed stability. Riley knew that. But April? She was just… April. How could he ignore what was happening between them?

She shook her head firmly. Sadness almost emanated from her pores. 'Oh, no. This could never be about Finn.' Tears glazed her eyes. 'He's perfect, Riley. He just is.'

'So what is it, then?'

She pulled a face. 'I'm going to say the corniest thing in the world. But, right now, it's just so true.'

He didn't speak. This was confusing him more by the second.

'It's not you, Riley. It's me.'

He let out an exasperated gasp. 'Oh, no. I'm not taking that.'

'There's so much you don't know.'

'Then tell me.' His voice was firm.

She was staring at him with those big blue eyes. 'My si-sister died,' she stuttered.

He stopped. It seemed an odd thing to say. 'I know that,' he said steadily. 'And I know this time of year is hard for everyone.'

She shook her head. 'My *twin* sister died.' Her hand was clasped around that charm.

It took him a few seconds. 'Your twin sister?'

She nodded.

'Identical twin?'

She nodded again.

It was cold out here—freezing. But Riley had the horrible sensation that he'd just been plunged into icy depths. Ovarian cancer. That was what she'd said Mallory died from. She'd mentioned she was young. She'd used the term 'unlucky'.

Twins. How much did he know about twins? How similar were their genes? Something clicked

in his head. Her necklace. Two hearts linked together. He felt a wave of panic. 'April, do you
have cancer?'

She shook her head. 'No. Well, I don't think
so. Not yet.'

Her voice sounded detached.

Thoughts were flooding through his brain. He'd
seen the reports. It might not be his speciality but
he couldn't miss the headlines from a few years
ago about the famous actress. They were making discoveries about cancer all the time. But this
was the one that had been given the most news
coverage. 'April, do you have the gene?'

She let out a sob and he pulled her towards him.
His brain was doing overtime. Trying to remember everything he'd ever heard. He could already
guess that her statistics wouldn't be great.

There were thick flakes of snow on her blue
coat. The outside of her was freezing. But he
didn't care. He could feel her trembling against
him. He hugged her even tighter and bent his
lips to her ear. 'There's things that can be done.
Have you seen someone? Have you spoken to a
counsellor?'

Her words were low. 'I've done all that. I know

my chances. My surgery will happen in the New Year.'

He pulled back, surprised, and put both hands on her face. He couldn't believe she'd been helping him so much while going through something like this.

'January? April, I had no idea. I'm so sorry. Why didn't you tell me?'

Another tear slid down her face. 'How do I tell someone that? How do I say, *Nice to meet you, but I'm a carrier of a potentially deadly gene, I'm going for surgery soon and I won't be able to have children.* I'm never going to get to be a mum. And maybe I won't even be here. The surgery isn't a guarantee. I might still go on and develop cancer at some stage. And yes, I have looked at all my options. It's all I've thought about for months.'

He lifted his thumb and wiped away her warm tear. He couldn't even begin to comprehend what she'd been going through. He'd been so focused on himself, and on Finn. He hadn't really left room for anything else. He hated himself right now. He'd known there was something he couldn't put his finger on. He should have pressed her. He should have pushed harder and let her share the burden, let her talk things over.

Her head was against his chest. 'I'm sorry. I didn't want to tell you. I didn't want to tell anyone. I need to get this over with. I need to have my surgery, get out the other side, then see what comes next. I just needed some time. I just needed a chance to—'

He pulled her back again. 'A chance to what? To be alone?' He shook his head. 'You don't need to do that. You don't need to be on your own, April.'

She sucked in a deep breath as she pulled herself free of his grasp. But he wasn't quite ready to let her go. He put his hands on her shoulders. 'But I do, Riley. This is hard. This—' she held up her hand '—whatever it could be, it just isn't the right time.' She met his gaze. 'And it isn't for you either. You have Finn to think of. You have to concentrate on him.'

'I know I do,' he had to stop himself from snapping. 'But Finn likes you. I like you. I don't want this to go away, April. I want to see what *this* is. I want to know.'

Her lips were trembling. She lifted her hand

and put it over his. 'We both work in the medical profession. Let's be clear about this. I think I'm well right now. I hope I'm well. But until I have my surgery, and until I have my pathology report, we just don't know. What if I'm not okay? What if I'm riddled with cancer? You've just introduced me to Finn. He's lost his mum. He's a five-year-old kid who just had to stand at his mother's funeral. What kind of person would I be if I didn't consider Finn here?'

It was like a fist closing around Riley's heart. Protect. That should be his first parental responsibility. As much as he hated every word, she was making sense.

'I could be in an accident tomorrow, just like Isabel was.' They were the first words that came into his brain. He knew they sounded desperate. But that was how he was feeling right now.

She shook her head. 'I know that. But it's a cop-out. You need to give me some space. You need to spend time with Finn and leave me out of the equation.' She tipped back her head and let out an ironic laugh. 'I knew from the first second that I saw you that you'd be trouble. I tried so hard to stay out of your way—and it almost worked.'

Something swelled inside his chest. 'You did? You deliberately kept away from me?'

'Of course I did.' She was smiling as she shook her head.

'Darn it. I thought my spider sense had stopped working. I thought you didn't like me at all.' The pathetic thing was that her words gave his male sensibilities a real sense of pride. He hadn't imagined things. She'd felt the attraction as much as he had.

Her hand was still over his and he gave her shoulders a squeeze. His stomach was churning. He didn't know enough about this condition. He only knew the bare basics and statistics he'd heard in casual conversations with other professionals. All of a sudden he wanted to know so much more.

'I don't want you to be alone through all of this, April. Let me be your friend.'

Her voice was shaky. 'I don't even know if we should do that.'

'Why?'

She winced. 'Riley, you're buying a house. A beautiful family home. In a few years, once you and Finn are settled, you'll want to fill that house with more children. I can already see what a good dad you are. It's a steep learning curve. But you're getting there. And you will thrive doing this, Riley. You will.'

'And?' He didn't get where she was going with this.

Another tear slid down her face. 'And once I have the surgery, my ovaries are removed. My fallopian tubes are gone. I can't have kids of my own. I can't have kids with you. The option is gone. And I'm not going to change my mind about this. The disease is such a silent killer they haven't really found any reliable way to monitor for it yet. I can't live with a perpetual cancer cloud over my head. I won't. But I also don't want to take the chance of children away from you. Finn should have the chance to have brothers and sisters. At some point you'll want to fill that house with children, Riley, and I can't do that with you.'

He shook his head. 'You...we don't know any of that yet. And you must have thought about this. There's other ways to have kids. You must have considered that in your future.'

She pressed her hand over her heart. 'There is.

And that's the option for me.' She lifted her hand and pressed it against his chest. 'But it doesn't have to be the option for you.'

There was so much swirling around in his head right now. He'd just had the best kiss of his life. A kiss that seemed perfect. A kiss that told him everything he thought he needed to know.

And now it seemed that kiss could result in a life he couldn't quite add up in his head. Finn had been a big enough shock. Families and kids had always seemed in his distant future. Filling a house with kids seemed a bit Neanderthal, but was he really willing to write all that off after a kiss? And what if April was sick or did get sick? What could that do to Finn? How much could one kid take?

April must have read all the confusion on his face. It was like watching a shield come down. A protective barrier.

'Concentrate on Christmas. Concentrate on Finn.' Her voice sounded tight.

He reached up to touch her cheek again but she stepped back. Her hair was coated with snow. She must be freezing right now. And even though his brain was telling him to take some time, to think about things, his heart was telling him something else entirely.

'And give me a little space at work,' she added.

His mouth opened to respond. He didn't want to give her space. But she held up her hand. 'Please, Riley.' She pressed her lips together. 'Now, I have work to do.'

She turned and headed off through the heavily falling snow to the other ward.

And left his broken heart somewhere out in the snow.

CHAPTER NINE

IT HAD FELT like the longest day in the world. She'd held it together as long as she could but as April walked into her flat and turned on the side lamp she felt exhaustion overwhelm her.

The mask she'd worn all day on her face finally slipped and the pent-up tears started to fall again.

Her Christmas tree was in the corner of the room. It was black with purple baubles and lights. When she'd bought it a few years ago black trees had been very avant-garde. But those days were long gone, and now it just felt a bit pretentious.

She sagged down onto the sofa. She'd loved this flat since she'd bought it after getting the job at Waterloo Court. But as she sat in the dimly lit room, watching the flickering purple lights and staring out into the dark night outside, for the first time it seemed so empty.

She'd always unconsciously smiled when she got back home. She'd felt warmth walking into her own place. She quite liked staying on her own. It was nice not to have to wrestle the duvet off someone else, or fight over the remote control.

Or was it?

A tear prickled in the corner of her eye. She'd been a twin. She *was* a twin. Mallory had been an integral part of her. When they'd reached their teenage years both had chosen separate university and career paths. Both had created their own circle of friends. But they'd still had each other.

That teenage resentment which had flared for around five minutes had rapidly disappeared. They'd started to appreciate each other more. Their university campuses had been two hundred miles apart but April had spent more time speaking to her sister on the phone than they'd spoken in the last few years sharing a room at home.

There were still mornings when she woke and, for a few brief seconds, she thought her sister was still alive. Then realisation hit all over again.

She couldn't pick up the phone and hear Mallory's voice at the other end. She couldn't hear about her latest date. The latest fight at work.

Mallory had left this life as she'd entered. With April by her side.

April had climbed into the hospice bed alongside her sister and just held her as her mother and father had sat on either side.

April wiped the tear from her eye. She rested her head back against the sofa. If only she could talk to her sister about the genetic tests. The surgery. The family that she'd always hoped for but would now never have.

Today, everything she'd kept tightly locked inside, everything she hadn't talked about to anyone but her parents, had come bubbling to the surface.

Her finger touched her lips and she closed her eyes.

That kiss. For a few moments, a few seconds, things had been perfect.

Life had been what it should be.

The gorgeous, sexy guy who had flirted with her and teased her, tangled his way around her heart, had kissed her in a way that had made every single part of her feel alive again.

Every nerve ending had sparked, lit up by the sensation of his lips on hers. It was better than she'd ever even imagined. And she might have imagined quite a bit.

But it had broken her heart more than she ever could have contemplated.

Her actions felt selfish. But she wasn't being selfish.

She didn't want to make promises to Riley that she couldn't keep. She had to be upfront. She had to be honest. She didn't want to form a relationship with the gorgeous man and little boy that could ultimately hurt them all.

She wanted him to be happy. She wanted Finn to be happy.

But ever since she'd met him she'd been so confused. Living in her own little box had seemed to simplify things for her. Gene testing. Decision. Surgery.

Then…

She pulled her knees up to her chest and hugged them tight.

She'd never felt so alone.

First Mallory. Then Riley. Now Finn.

Her stomach twinged again and she rubbed it to ease the pain.

Her mind was as foggy as the weather outside. And she just couldn't see a way through.

Finn was sleeping by seven o'clock. He'd said school was busy and he was tired.

Riley was distracted. He couldn't concentrate. His mind had been full of what April had told him.

He set up his computer and began researching.

He read and read and read. Everything he could find out about BRCA1 and BRCA2. Finding out the risks for twins was much more difficult. There was limited research.

BRCA1 genetic mutation was scary. April had mentioned something about a strong family history and, considering her sister had already died, he had to assume there had been some other ovarian cancer cases in her family too. There was also the added risk of breast cancers—although she hadn't mentioned that. At least for breast cancer, there was an evidence-based screening programme that could pick up early signs. Ovarian cancer was much more difficult.

The hours just seemed to meld together, his concentration only broken by some mumbles from Finn's room. He walked through. Finn seemed restless and Riley sat at the edge of the bed and stroked his hair. 'Hey, little guy, it's okay. Go back to sleep.'

'Dad,' came the muffled voice. He smiled at that. It warmed his heart. There would always be that tiny sense of resentment that he hadn't seen Finn get to this stage. When his mother had visited she'd voiced her opinion about Isabel's decision over and over once Finn had gone to bed. And he did understand, but it also made him appreciate how unhelpful that was.

'Is April here?'

Riley was jerked from his thoughts. He lowered his head down next to Finn's. 'What?'

Finn still looked as if he were sleeping. 'I miss April,' he murmured.

It was as if the little voice tugged directly on his heart. 'I miss her too' was his immediate response. He'd seen her today. He'd kissed her today. He'd held her today. And she'd revealed the deepest, darkest secret that she'd been keeping for so long.

It felt as if he'd failed her. Completely and utterly failed her.

The conversation kept playing back in his head but each time with different scenarios. He'd said something different; he'd done something different. He'd told her how much she meant to him. He'd told her he wanted to help her through all this.

His stomach curled again as he looked at his sleeping son. He was so peaceful. So settled. This might be the honeymoon period. The social worker had told him that Isabel's death could affect him in a whole host of different ways that might manifest over time.

He squeezed his eyes closed. What if the surgery wasn't soon enough for April? What if she was already sick and just didn't know it yet?

His hand kept stroking Finn's head. He felt physically sick now. Her risk of particular cancers was still higher. Getting rid of her ovaries and fallopian tubes would not be the all-clear. But it would reduce her risk of dying of ovarian cancer by eighty per cent. That was massive. After surgery, it would be about learning to manage the risks.

He wanted to be by her side. He didn't want her to go through any of this alone.

But what about his son?

He would be making a decision that could leave his son vulnerable. They could both put their hearts on the line, loving someone who could possibly be sick at some point.

It was a risk he was willing to take for himself, but could he really do that for his son?

He sighed and lay down next to Finn. There wasn't a parenting book in the world that would cover this one.

CHAPTER TEN

'IS THAT OUR new house?' Finn's voice echoed from the back of the car as they pulled up outside.

Riley wanted to smile. He did. Even from here he had a good feeling about this place. 'Yes, it is.'

Finn waved something from the back of the car. 'We still have to give this to April, Dad.'

Riley nodded. Finn had made a card at school for April yesterday. It had melted his heart and he just wasn't sure what to do with it.

'No problem. We'll do that later.'

He glanced down at the keys in his hand as his mobile sounded.

His mother had organised things with military precision. The sofa, beds, TV, fridge freezer, washing machine and dryer were all arriving in the next few hours. Money just seemed to have haemorrhaged from his bank account in the last few days. He looked down at the message. It seemed that the engineer would be here in the next hour to connect the Internet and cable TV.

He jumped out of the car and unclipped Finn's seat belt. 'Come on, little guy. Let's go pick a bedroom.'

The rest of the car was jam-packed with bedding, towels and kitchen paraphernalia. He hadn't even started trying to get their clothes together.

Finn skipped up the path. This was odd. In his head he'd sort of imagined April being next to them when this happened. The key turned easily in the lock and he pushed the door open.

He'd rented this place without even setting foot in it. But it seemed his instincts had been spot on. People always said you knew within thirty seconds if a house was for you or not; Riley didn't need that long.

They walked from room to room. After army housing the space just seemed enormous. Two people could never fill this place.

His stomach rolled. April's eyes appeared in his head. The sorrow in them when she'd mentioned this place and how she could imagine it filled in the future.

But although he could see it in a few years,

filled with his touches and decorated the way he wanted, he couldn't imagine the anonymous wife that April could, or the nameless children. The only person he could see here was April.

She'd avoided him the last few days. He knew that. Of course he knew that. And even though she'd insisted he give her some space, his heart wouldn't really let him comply. He'd sent her a text. And left a phone message. Just saying he was thinking about her. Because he was. And Finn was too. Even if she didn't want to know that right now.

He didn't like this distance between them. Every cell in his body told him that it was wrong. But he wanted to respect her request. He didn't want to force himself and Finn on her if that wasn't something she could cope with right now.

Because this wasn't all about him.

The thought sent a memory shooting through him. April, saying almost those exact words to him when they'd sat in the coffee shop together. He hadn't understood at the time. He'd still been at that jokey, flirty stage then. It seemed like a lifetime ago.

Then there had been that kiss in the garden

centre. The one where she'd told him it wasn't the right time.

She hadn't been talking about the garden centre at all. She'd been talking about now. Now was not the right time for April. Now he understood—even if he didn't really agree.

Finn ran up the stairs, darting from room to room. 'This one—no, this one. No, this one!'

Riley smiled. Finn could have any room he wanted. He walked through to the dining room that looked out over the back garden. A football goal—that was what he could put out there for Finn. The garden was much longer than he'd anticipated. A lawnmower—he'd need to get one. Something he'd never owned and never even considered. Thank goodness it was winter and the grass wasn't growing. The whole place was covered in snow and ice; it looked like something from a kid's book.

Somehow things just didn't feel right. He'd imagined April somewhere in this picture. But she'd made it clear she wasn't ready for that—and he was trying so hard to respect her wishes right now.

He sighed and turned back to the living room.

The large sash windows with internal shutters were exactly what he'd expected in a house like this. His mother had even ordered blinds for the windows, but they wouldn't arrive until tomorrow.

His mother was doing better than he'd anticipated. He knew she wanted to be here—he knew she wanted to smother Finn. But, for once, she was listening. And giving her a range of tasks to do that would benefit Finn seemed to have played to her strengths. He was starting to appreciate her tenaciousness in a way he'd never imagined.

The previous owner had left a pile of wood next to the fireplace. It made him laugh as the 'living flame' fire was actually gas. He walked over and bent down to light it. It didn't matter that it was the middle of the day and the house was warm enough already. He needed some more heat. He wanted the place to seem more cosy. Because right now the emptiness echoed around him.

A white van with green writing pulled up outside. He smiled. Perfect. The most ridiculous thing to do first in the new house. He couldn't have planned it better.

'Finn, come on down! The Christmas tree is

here,' he shouted. He'd persuaded the garden centre to delay their delivery until they arrived at the house. Sure enough, the guys were already bringing the boxes with the decorations to the door.

Finn squealed and ran down the stairs, throwing the front door wide to the world and letting the icy-cold air blast in around them.

Riley gave a nod to the delivery guys. 'Welcome to the mad house,' he said.

This was going to be a long, long day.

It was later than she expected. But the last few days April hadn't been in a hurry to get home from work. So she'd taken a few of the patients down to the gym for an extra session after dinner. They'd started an impromptu game of wheelchair basketball and she'd been dumped out of her chair on at least three occasions.

She knew she was safe. Riley wasn't working today. This was the day he got the keys to the house. The place that he and Finn would call home.

She wanted to be happy for him. It was a gorgeous house. A perfect place. Her own flat paled in comparison. And she hated that, because she used to love it.

Her stomach gave yet another twinge as she righted the chair and shook herself down. 'That's it for me, guys. You've finished me.'

They laughed. The camaraderie in here was one of the best parts of the job. Everyone looking out for each other. She was sure if she shared with her colleagues her plans for surgery they would be more than supportive. Of course they would. But it was coming up to Christmas. She didn't want to have those kinds of chats. Maybe in the New Year when she knew her surgery date she'd start to tell a few people.

The guys left and she finished tidying up the gym before turning the lights out, grabbing her coat and heading for home.

The snow seemed to be heavier yet again. She pulled her hat down over her ears and fastened the top button on her coat.

Her stomach growled. Food. There was little in the fridge. Maybe she should get a takeaway? She groaned. She'd forgotten her purse today. She'd have to go home first and pick it up.

As she pushed her front door open, she almost trod on an envelope that was bright red with squiggly writing on the front. She picked it up. *ApRiL*. Her heart lurched. It was obviously a child's writing, a mixture of upper- and lower-case letters, and she could almost imagine Finn's tongue sticking out at the side of his mouth as he'd tried his hardest at writing. It couldn't possibly be from anyone else.

She blinked back tears as she pulled the handmade card out of the envelope. There were a few things stuck on the card. A silver foil star. A green, badly cut out tree along with something else in yellow she couldn't quite distinguish. Baubles were drawn at the edges of the tree in red pencil, and another wiggly blue pencil line snaked up the tree, representing the lights or the tinsel. Her heart gave a tug as she remembered the blue lights that he'd picked.

She opened the card.

To my fiend.
Love Finn

She laughed. She couldn't help it. She loved the fact he'd missed the R.

It was beautiful. It was sorrowful. She could

imagine how long he'd taken to make this for her. But it was also joyful. She hugged the card against her chest, wishing it was both Riley and Finn.

She blinked back the tears as she walked over to her shelf and put Finn's Christmas card in front of all the others. It had pride of place for her. She wanted to look at it and remind herself what could be out there when she was ready.

Her stomach growled loudly again and she grabbed her purse, which was lying on her sofa. The walk to the main street only took a few minutes.

She loved the winter time—especially when the pavements were glistening and the trees were dusted with snow. The lamp posts glowed orange, bathing the rest of the street in a warm hue. Even though it was after seven, the hustle and bustle of Christmas shopping was alive and well on the high street. All of the shops had started opening late, enticing people to shop more and more.

Some of the takeaways already had queues but her eyes were drawn to the soft yellow lights from the old church. She smiled. From here it looked like the church from the Christmas village in the garden centre. There were sandwich boards on the pavement outside. *Christmas Cheer Dinner*. She'd forgotten about that.

She rubbed her hands together as she glanced at the queue outside the pizza shop. She'd been introduced to the Christmas Cheer Dinner last year by a colleague. The church members chose one night to make a proper Christmas dinner that everyone could attend and pay what they wished. It was really a charity fundraiser, allowing them to use the proceeds from that night to make an actual Christmas dinner for those in the homeless hostels on Christmas Day. She'd planned on eating at home, alone. It might be nice to eat amongst some other people and donate to the cause.

Her feet carried her into the church hall automatically. She smiled at a few familiar faces and joined the queue of people waiting for dinner. There was a choir from the local school singing some carols in a corner of the room, with a few playing instruments. She couldn't help but smile. Christmas was always all about the kids. The biggest tree she'd ever seen was in another corner, adorned with red and gold decorations, and small tea lights were on the window ledges beneath the stained-glass windows, sending streams of red, blue and green across the room.

The line moved quickly and she soon had a plate with a steaming-hot Christmas dinner and she stuffed a few notes into the collection pot next to the cutlery.

She looked around. There was a low hum of chatter amongst the people already eating dinner. Most of the tables were full, with only a few spaces here and there. The lights at the food dispensary were bright, but the lights in the hall were dim; the tables had flickering candles lining them, creating a more Christmas-like atmosphere.

She walked over to the table nearest the choir. It would be nice to hear the children sing as she ate.

'April!' came the shout.

She recognised the voice instantly. Finn was in the front line of the choir—how had she missed that cheeky face?—and he looked as proud as Punch dressed in his uniform of grey trousers and a red jumper. 'There's a space next to Dad. You can see me!'

April gulped and looked to where an excited

Finn was pointing. Riley glanced up from his plate of turkey and gave her a half-smile and shrug. He'd texted and left her a message a few days ago but she hadn't responded. She'd spent the last two days timing her visits to wards to ensure they didn't coincide with his. But she couldn't keep doing this.

Her heart gave a lurch as she sat down next to him.

'Sorry,' he murmured.

'It's fine,' she said, giving Finn a wave. 'I had no idea he was singing with the choir.'

'Neither had I,' sighed Riley. 'I found the note in his school bag about five minutes after the last delivery guy left.' He gave a wry smile. 'Remind me in future that I need to check the school bag every day. There were four notes in there.'

April smiled as she tried not to look into those green eyes. It had only been a few days and she missed them—no matter how much she'd tried not to.

She picked up her knife and fork. 'I'd forgotten about the Christmas Cheer Dinner. I came last year too. Couldn't eat for about three days after it because the portions here are huge.' She glanced sideways. Riley's eyes were locked on hers.

'How are you?' he said quietly.

She broke their gaze and looked down at her food. 'I'm fine,' she said automatically. She paused. 'Thank you for the card. It was lovely. It was so thoughtful.' She looked up at Finn, who automatically gave her another wave.

'He missed you.' Riley's voice was hoarse. 'I miss you too.'

As she stared at her dinner her appetite started to leave her. She moved her knife and fork; it would be a shame to waste this lovely dinner. She didn't want to get upset. She'd come in here tonight because it felt like the right place to be. She wanted to help the charitable cause, and she wanted to surround herself with people who loved Christmas as much as she did.

She started eating. People around them were chatting easily. The kids started another song. One of the helpers came around and filled up all their glasses.

The words *I miss you both too* reverberated around her brain. She really, really wanted to say them. It felt honest to say them. But something still stopped her.

'How was the house move?' she asked quickly.

For a second it seemed as if Riley's face fell, as if he'd been waiting for her to say something else. But he gave a brief nod. 'Exhausting. I didn't know I could plumb in a washing machine, but apparently I can. I had to go and knock on a neighbour's door to get him to help me lift the TV onto the wall.'

'You bought one of those giant TVs?' She was smiling. She couldn't help it.

'Of course I did.' He gestured towards Finn. 'The cable and Internet guy arrived this morning. It's the first time I've ever paid for cable TV in my life. I was living in hope of endless nights of watching the sports channels, but it seems Finn has other plans entirely.'

She swallowed her food. 'He found the cartoon channels, didn't he?'

Riley raised his eyebrows and nodded, folding his arms across his chest. 'Boy, did he. Do you have any idea how many kids' TV channels there are?'

She laughed. 'Oh, yes. I had an introduction the other night. We should compare lists.'

He met her smile. 'We should, shouldn't we?'

Their gazes meshed again. It was almost as if the world fell silent around them. The hum of voices blocked out. It was just him. And her. In the flickering candlelight.

Riley. The guy who had well and truly captured her heart. She couldn't deny it a second longer. She hadn't meant to fall in love. She absolutely hadn't. But it seemed that fate had other ideas for her.

And it wasn't just Riley she'd fallen in love with. It was Finn too. They were a package deal.

She'd never hated her genes more than she hated them now. Not even when they'd stolen her sister from her. The thought made her catch her breath.

She wanted to move on with her life. She wanted to feel as if she could plan for the future. Her fingers actually itched to pull her phone from her pocket and demand a surgery date right now. Once she'd had the surgery she might feel as if she could take stock. To sit down with Riley and talk about the possibility of a future together—if he still wanted that.

She'd seen the fleeting worry on his face when she'd mentioned Finn the other day. Maybe that worry had planted seeds and grown? If it had, there was nothing she could do. She'd never do anything to hurt Riley and Finn.

But, if that was the case, why was he telling her that he missed her?

She couldn't pull her gaze away from his. She wanted to stay right here, in this moment, for the rest of her life.

It was like being in a bubble. A place where no one was under threat of being sick. Christmas was captured, Finn was happy and there was time just for the two of them. Why couldn't she just stay here?

Riley's hand closed over hers, sending a wave of tingles up her arm. 'This won't ever go away, will it?' she breathed, half questioning, half hopeful.

He lifted one hand and put it behind her head, pulling her closer to him. 'I don't want it to,' he whispered as his lips met hers.

It didn't matter that they were in the middle of

the church hall. It didn't matter that people were on either side of them. It was just the simplest and sweetest of kisses. Nothing more. Nothing less. But it filled her with a warmer glow than any fire or candle could.

The music changed around them, a more modern tune bellowing from the speakers. Riley pulled back, smiling. 'Since when is "Jingle Bell Rock" a Christmas carol?' he asked.

She laughed and put her head on his shoulder, just taking a few seconds to breathe in his scent and remind herself what she was doing. Their little bubble had vanished. But she didn't mind. The kids had all been handed out tambourines and were banging away to their own beat. Riley pulled out his phone to video Finn for his mum. 'If I send her this it will keep her happy. She's coming down in a few days to apparently "sort the house out". I might come and hide at yours.'

He slid his arm around her shoulders as they watched Finn and his classmates singing. Tears glistened in her eyes. 'He's doing so well, Riley. He really is.'

'He'll do even better if he thinks you'll be

around,' Riley replied. 'We both will.' He sounded so determined. So sure.

Her heart skipped a few beats. This was what she wanted. It had just seemed so far away. So impossible right now.

She closed her eyes for a second and sent a silent prayer upwards.

Please let this be for real. Please.

CHAPTER ELEVEN

EVERYTHING FELT GOOD. Everything felt right.

It didn't matter that the house was still organised chaos. It didn't matter that he'd spent twenty minutes this morning trying to find one of Finn's school shoes. All that mattered was that he finally felt as if things were on the right track with April.

He'd made a few more casual enquiries about jobs. It seemed that the GP track would be the most viable for him, and the more he considered it, the more interested he became. All the clinics that he'd ever done in settings overseas had been walk-ins. It meant he'd had to deal with a wide range of different issues—a bit like GPs did here. Sure, there had been a whole host of area-specific complications, but it wouldn't be as big a jump as he'd first thought.

Finn had been so animated last night. He'd been so happy that April had watched him sing with the choir and when he'd finished she'd made a fuss of him. She hadn't gone home with them last night, but they'd walked her back to her flat and she'd given them both a kiss on the cheek.

It might not have seemed like enough. But it was enough for right now.

He looked around the ward again. April hadn't appeared yet today. He glanced at his watch. It was coming up to lunchtime. She must be at the other ward. He would go and find her and see if he could interest her in some lunch.

April hadn't walked home last night—she'd glided. At least that was what it felt like. When she'd finally gone to bed she thought it was just nervous excitement that meant she couldn't sleep. It didn't take long to realise it was more than that.

For the last few weeks she'd had weird occasional grumblings in her stomach. Sometimes it felt like indigestion, leaving her feeling nauseous and sick. She was used to having painful periods. Her doctor had put her on the oral contraceptive pill to help reduce her risk of ovarian cancer and also to help with her painful periods.

But the period pain had continued. But this type of pain felt different.

She'd shifted around in bed all night, finally getting up to take some painkillers, then getting up an hour later to try to drink some tea.

It hadn't helped. She'd finally pulled on her uniform and gone into work as normal. But as the morning progressed, so did her pain.

John Burns had even commented on her colour as she worked with him. 'Hope you're not coming down with something. Last thing I need is a sickness bug. You're a terrible colour.'

She'd made her excuses and left, going to the ladies' bathroom and retching in the sink.

Her skin broke out in beads of sweat. But the beads of sweat were cold. She shivered as the pain swept through her abdomen again. She ran into the cubicle and sat down, bolting the door.

The sweating wouldn't stop. She could feel it running between her shoulder blades. But it was the waves of pain that were worse.

She put her head against the side of the cubicle as she doubled over in pain. Horror swept through her. Her stomach felt rigid.

Mallory's had been bloated. But she'd had a

whole host of other symptoms. Unusual bleed-ing. Nausea. Pain in her abdomen, pelvis, back and legs. Indigestion. And a complete and utter feeling of exhaustion.

Now, she thought she might be sick again. Her stomach wasn't bloated. She hadn't had any strange bleeding, or pain in her back or legs. But she had felt nauseous a number of times over the last few weeks. There had also been niggling pains—nothing like today, of course.

But now she felt gripped with panic. She'd been so distracted these last few weeks. All because of Riley and Finn. They'd captured her attention. Made her less vigilant.

She'd had a few tiny thoughts when she'd felt the niggles of pain. But she'd been used to painful periods and just put it down to that. She hadn't been tired, or bloated, so it had seemed over the top to start panicking.

But right now she'd never felt pain like it.

She should never have kissed Riley. She should never have started to feel attached to Finn. What if she was sick? Riley had enough to cope with, learning to be a father. Finn didn't need some-one to enter his life, then leave him alone again.

He was just a kid. He didn't deserve that. A hot, angry tear spilled down her cheek.

She pushed herself up and opened the cubicle door again.

This was a hospital. It might not have an accident and emergency department, but it had enough doctors that someone would be able to take a look at her.

She tried to straighten up, but her abdomen didn't really agree.

Catching sight of herself in the mirror didn't help. There were black circles under her eyes, only highlighted by the paleness of her skin.

She opened the door back into the corridor.

Riley was standing directly opposite, talking to someone in the corridor and showing them his phone. 'The pictures are great—the house looks fabulous.' The nurse smiled and gave him a nudge. 'And big. I take it at some point you'll be planning on using all those rooms?'

April froze and Riley gave a casual response. 'Yeah…maybe.'

She already knew it was time to walk away. She didn't want Riley and Finn to see her sick.

But that? That was just the extra push that she needed.

Riley looked up. 'Hey, there you are. I've been looking for you. Want to go and get some lunch?'

She shook her head and did her best to walk in the opposite direction. She didn't even want to have this conversation. Her brain was so mixed up. Last night she'd been so happy. Things that had seemed out of her reach were right in front of her. She should have known it was too good to be true.

Why should she get to live the life that Mallory didn't? They'd come into this world together— maybe they should have gone out of it together.

Her head was swimming. She couldn't think straight. Irrational thoughts were filling her head.

'Hey—' Riley stepped in front of her '—is something wrong?'

He seemed to blur in her vision. His voice seemed far away, even though he was right in front of her. 'Go away, Riley. Go away. This isn't going to work. It was never going to work. I asked you to give me some space.' She stopped. The wave of pain made her want to double over again.

'April—' this time his voice was directly in her ear '—April, what's wrong?'

She shook her head. She couldn't do this. If she was ill, she didn't want Riley to feel as if he had to be around her. There was enough going on in his life. He didn't need a sick girlfriend, and she couldn't bear for him to see her the way her sister had ended up. A shadow of her former self, weak, emaciated, in constant pain and finally wishing her life away. It had broken April's heart. It had broken her mum's and dad's hearts. She didn't want him to stay with her out of duty or some kind of responsibility.

But, more importantly, she didn't want him to stay with her out of love.

That would break her heart as much as his and Finn's.

She had to walk away. She had to be strong and determined.

She pulled herself straight, willing herself to forget the waves of pain just for a few seconds.

'I'm sorry, Riley. We should never have got involved. It was wrong of me. It was wrong of you. Finn needs your full attention.' She took a deep breath. 'And I'm not sure if I could ever love someone else's son the way I should.' She hated those words. Every single one of them was a lie. But pushing Riley away now was so much more important than him feeling indebted to her when she finally got the diagnosis she was dreading.

Why hadn't her last lot of bloods shown the CA125 antigen? Why hadn't she acted sooner? Why had she wasted time?

Right now she was angry with herself. But she still cared about Riley and Finn. She didn't want them to have to take this path with her.

Riley's face was pale. 'April, what on earth are you talking about? What's changed between now and last night? Have I missed something?'

'No,' she answered abruptly. 'But I have. Let's just leave it. Let's just not take things any further.'

She was trying her absolute best to hold things together. She could see the hurt in his eyes. She knew this was really what neither of them wanted.

He grabbed hold of her arm. 'Wait a minute. You don't mean this.'

She met his gaze. 'You were just a distraction for me, Riley. A chance to not think about things. And, let's face it, I was just a distraction for you too. I can't give you what you want. We both know that.' She couldn't pretend that she hadn't heard those words he'd just said to the nurse.

Confusion swept over his face. He looked as if she'd just punched him in the chest. 'Finn,' he stuttered. 'You think you can't love Finn?' The cruel words had obviously stuck in his head. He looked shell-shocked.

'No. I can't.'

She pushed past him. She had to get out of here. She had to get away from him and find someone who could help her get to the bottom of this pain.

She walked as quickly as she could, her whole body shaking. Riley would hate her now, almost as much as she hated herself.

Maybe that was for the best.

She pushed open the door to the courtyard. The cold wind took the breath from her body just as another wave of pain hit.

The last thing she remembered was the white snow coming up to greet her.

Riley was stunned. At first he'd thought April was unwell. Her colour was terrible and she'd looked in pain.

But maybe he'd imagined it? Because when she looked directly into his eyes and told him she'd made a mistake and she couldn't love Finn it had felt like a knife stabbing through his heart.

This wasn't the woman that he knew. This wasn't the caring, compassionate and supportive woman that he'd spent time with over the last few weeks. The woman who had stolen his heart and helped him reassess his life. Nothing about this felt right. He loved her. He just hadn't told her that yet.

And it looked as if he wouldn't be telling her that now.

How on earth could he be with someone who proclaimed they didn't have the ability to love his son? They were a package. Nothing would come between them. He couldn't let it.

His feet were rooted to the spot as she walked away.

Finn. He had to focus on Finn. Maybe he just hadn't taken the time to get to know April properly. He'd been so caught up in being a good father to Finn, and acting on the attraction between them both, that he hadn't really taken time to step back and think about the future.

His breath caught in his throat. That was a lie. He *had* thought about the future. He'd contemplated the words that April had said to him about the possibility of being sick. He'd sat next to Finn and wondered if he should take things forward.

Guilt swept over him. Of course he had. But surely it was his duty to Finn to consider these things and how they might affect him? Was that really why he hadn't told April that he loved her?

It didn't matter that he'd pushed those thoughts aside. It didn't matter that even though he'd still been worried, the thought of not having April in their lives had seemed like a much more difficult concept than dealing with the fact she could get sick.

The truth was any one of them could get sick. Riley, Finn or April. Life was about taking risks. Taking the safe route could mean that he and Finn would miss out on so much more.

That was what he'd believed. That was what he'd thought after a long and sleepless night.

So why hadn't he just told her? That he and Finn wanted April in their lives full stop.

'Help!' The shout came from down the corridor. Riley started running. It was one of the domestic staff—she was holding the door open to the courtyard. Two of the nurses came running from the other direction. And then he saw her.

April. Her body crumpled in the snow.

And he didn't think he could breathe again.

CHAPTER TWELVE

EVERYTHING WAS WHITE. Everything was too white.

Fear gripped her. Was this it?

Then she heard a noise. A shuffle of feet.

She turned her head. A nurse gave her a smile as she pressed a button and made a BP cuff inflate around April's arm. April grimaced. She'd seen this done a hundred times but she hadn't realised it made your arm feel as if it were going to fall off.

After a few uncomfortable minutes the cuff released. She looked around. She didn't recognise this place. 'Where am I?'

'Arlington General.' The nurse gave her another smile. 'I think you managed to give your work colleagues quite a fright. They've all been camped outside.' She checked the monitor once more. 'I'm going to go and tell the surgeon you're awake. He'll want to come and chat to you.' The nurse went to leave then pointed to something on the bedside table. 'Oh, someone left a present for you.' She gave an amused smile. 'Apparently it's very important.'

The nurse seemed relaxed as she left the room. April tried to move in bed, letting out a yelp. Her right side was still sore, but this was a different kind of pain.

Had the surgeon removed her ovary? She let her hand slip under the covers to feel her abdomen. She had some kind of dressing on her right side. Why would he remove one, and not the other? Surely it was better to do both at once?

She looked from side to side. Her mouth was dry and she couldn't see any water. There was a buzzer at the side of the bed but she didn't want to press it. The nurse had just been in; surely she would come back soon?

Her eyes fell on the parcel. She frowned. It didn't have the neatest wrapping she'd ever seen. But at least it was close enough to reach.

Yip. It looked like recycled wrapped paper, along with half a roll of sticky tape. She peeled away at a small piece of the paper that had managed to escape the sticky tape frenzy. It was something soft—very soft—and pink that was inside.

Now she was intrigued. What on earth was that?

There was a noise at the door.

She looked up. Riley. He was nervously hanging around the door. He looked pale. He looked as if he might have been crying.

Tears welled in her eyes. What she really wanted was a bear hug. But she couldn't ask for that. She wanted to hug it out like she and Mallory used to.

'The surgeon is coming,' she said hoarsely. 'I'm not sure that you should be here.'

He glanced over his shoulder and stepped inside. 'I know that. But I had to see you. I had to know if you were okay.'

She pressed her hand on her stomach. 'I don't know, Riley. I have no idea if I'm okay.'

He nodded and hovered around the side of the bed. 'They wouldn't tell me anything. I mean, of course they wouldn't tell me anything. I know they've phoned your mum and dad. They're on their way.'

'They are?' Now she was scared. She was truly

scared. They'd be coming down from Scotland in snowy weather. It probably wasn't the best idea, but if they were on their way, surely it only meant one thing.

The paper from the present crinkled in her other hand as it tightened around the parcel.

Riley glanced at the door again. 'It's from Finn. He said you needed it. He said it was important.' She looked down. She had no idea what it was.

'Riley, I…'

'Stop.' He moved forward and grabbed hold of her hand. 'I don't want you to talk. I just want you to listen.' She'd never seen him look so pale. 'I don't care what the surgeon tells you. Well, of course I care. But it won't change how I feel, and it won't change what I want to do.' He took a deep breath and paused. 'What I want *us* to do.'

She didn't even get a chance to respond.

'You're part of me, April. Whether you want to be or not. I know you said you need space. I know you said the timing isn't good for you. I didn't expect to find out I was a father and meet the woman I want to marry all in the space of a few weeks.' He held up one hand as he said the words. 'But too late. It's happened. And it's good. It's great. I can't pretend that it's anything else. I should have told you the other night. I should have told you at the Christmas Dinner. I don't know why I didn't. But I love you, April. Finn and I love you. Yes, things may be hard at times. Yes, we might take some time to get used to being a family. But I didn't believe you when you said you can't love Finn. I've seen it, April. I've seen it in your eyes. It's in every action you take, every move you make around him. You're good for him. And you're good for me.' He stopped talking for a second to catch his breath. 'Don't push us away. Don't. I am choosing to be part of your life. I am choosing for us to be part of your future. Whatever happens next, I want to be by your side. All you have to do is say yes.'

She couldn't breathe. How could this be happening?

Didn't he know what could lie ahead?

'You can't, Riley. You can't hang around. It's not fair.'

His voice became strong. 'What's not fair is meeting someone that you love and not being able to be with them. I want this, April.' He held up his hands. 'Whatever this may be, I want it.'

Tears pooled in her eyes.

He leaned closer. 'Tell me. Tell me if you love me and Finn. Be honest. If you don't, I can walk away. But I still won't leave you alone. I'll still be your friend. I'll still be around. But look me in the eye and tell me you don't feel the same way that I do.'

She felt her heart swell in her chest. Those green eyes were fixed straight on her. She could see the sincerity. She could see the strength. It was right there before her. His hand was still on hers. But he wasn't gripping her tightly. He was holding her gently, letting his thumb nuzzle into her palm.

She blinked back tears. 'I do love you, Riley. And of course I love Finn. But I just don't feel I've any right to. Not when I don't know what lies ahead.'

He bent forward and kissed her on the forehead then looked at their hands. 'Your hand in mine, April. That's the way we go forward. That's the way it's supposed to be.'

There was a noise at the door behind them. The surgeon cleared his throat and walked in. 'Everything okay in here?'

April nodded. Her mouth couldn't be any drier. She just wanted this part over with.

But as she waited to hear him speak she realised he didn't look the way she'd expected. He seemed almost jolly. The nurse came in too, holding a glass of water in her hand that she set on the bedside table.

He waved his hand. 'Chris Potter. I was the surgeon on call. You gave us quite a scare, lady.'

April swallowed. 'I did?'

He nodded and pointed to Riley. 'Okay to discuss things in front of your friend?'

Riley's grip tightened around her hand. 'Her fiancé,' he said quickly.

What? He'd just said what?

The surgeon didn't notice her surprise. He just carried on. 'It seems that you have quite a high pain threshold. Most people would have been at their GP's days ago with a grumbling appendix. You must have tolerated that for quite a few weeks. Unfortunately, you're one of the few that has gone on to develop acute appendicitis. Your appendix actually ruptured and you currently have peritonitis. You'll need to stay with us a few days for IV antibiotics. We need to ensure there's no chance of sepsis.'

It was like having an out-of-body experience. April was tempted to turn around to see if he was talking to someone else. Trouble was, she already knew the only thing behind her was a wall. There were no other patients in this room.

'My appendix?' she said quietly. Her brain was trying to process. And it was struggling. She hadn't imagined anything so…so—ordinary. Her mind had immediately gone to the worst-case scenario. There hadn't been room for anything else.

'Her appendix?' Riley said the words like a shout of joy. Then he must have realised how it looked and he tried to look serious again. 'So, that's it. Nothing else?'

The surgeon narrowed his eyes for a second, then nodded. 'I've seen your notes, Ms Henderson. I'm assuming you thought it might be something else?'

She nodded weakly.

He shook his head. 'Had we known about the grumbling appendix, then your gynaecologist and I could have arranged to do surgery together.

Unfortunately, as it was an emergency, we didn't have your consent for any other procedure and your gynaecologist was unavailable. I'm afraid your other surgery will have to be scheduled as planned in the New Year. Another anaesthetic isn't ideal, but I didn't have any other option.'

'But...but you didn't notice anything suspicious?'

The surgeon sighed. It was obvious he understood her question. 'I'm not a gynaecologist. I'm a general surgeon, so it's not my speciality. But no, at the time, on the right side I didn't notice anything of concern. Nothing obvious, at least.'

It was amazing, the temporary relief she felt. Of course she knew things happened at a cellular level, but even the simple words 'nothing obvious' were almost like a balm. That, and the hand firmly connected to hers.

The surgeon gave a nod. 'So, at least another twenty-four hours of IV antibiotics. Then we can discharge you home on oral. I think you'll still be sore for a few days and, as I know you're a physio, I'd recommend you stay off work for at least six to eight weeks.' He raised his eyebrows. 'I know you healthcare personnel. Itchy feet. Always want to go back too soon.' He gave them both a wink. 'But those transverse abdominal muscles take a while to heal properly. I'm sure you both know that.'

He picked up her case notes and left. The nurse with him gave them a smile. 'I'll give you some time alone. April, your mum phoned. They're stuck in traffic but should be here in around an hour.' She picked up the observation chart and left too.

For a few seconds neither of them spoke. It was as if they were still trying to take the news in—to process it.

Riley's hand squeezed hers again. 'When can we breathe again?' he whispered.

She laughed, instantly regretting it as her stomach muscles spasmed in protest. She didn't quite know what to say. 'I guess now would be good,' she finally said.

Riley didn't hesitate. He leaned over the bed and gathered April firmly but gently, slipping his arms under her shoulders and hugging her loosely.

She was taken aback, but after a second slid

her arms around his neck and whispered in his ear, 'What are we doing?'

He pulled back with a smile, resting his forehead against hers. 'We're doing something that a good friend taught me. And we're doing it in honour of someone else. We're hugging it out.'

Her eyes instantly filled with tears. 'Oh.' Now she really was lost for words. He'd remembered. He'd remembered the one thing she always did with her sister.

He moved and the paper on the gift crackled— it had been caught between them.

Riley picked it up. 'You haven't managed to open this yet. I think you should or I know a little guy who'll be immensely offended.'

She nodded, pulling at the paper again to try to uncover what the pink fluffy thing was. It took some tugging, finally revealing her prize. She pulled it free. 'Bed socks?' she asked in surprise.

Riley nodded. 'Finn said you have cold feet. He was very insistent.' He raised his eyebrows. 'I'm beginning to wonder if my son knows you better than I do.'

She laughed as she shook her head, struck that

Finn had remembered. Then she frowned. 'You had bed socks?'

He shook his head. 'No, I had money. I just had to hand it over to Finn and let him spend it in a shop on the way here.'

She tried to push herself up the bed. 'Finn is here too?'

Riley nodded. 'Of course he is. Where else would he be?' He met her gaze again. 'We're family,' he said simply.

A tear slid down her cheek. Riley was proving again and again that he meant what he said. He was here. And she knew he'd still be here if she'd had a bad diagnosis instead of a good one.

Why was she trying to walk away from the two men who'd captured her heart?

She licked her lips and he lifted a glass of water with a straw, almost as if he'd read her mind. 'Here, the nurse left this for you. Take a sip.'

She took a sip of the water and closed her hand over his. 'We need to talk.'

He raised his eyebrows. 'Why do I feel as if I'm about to get into trouble?'

She smiled. 'Oh, because you are.'

He perched at the edge of the bed. 'Hit me with it.'

'You called yourself something when the surgeon was in. I don't think we've had a chance to talk about it.'

He nodded. 'Fiancé.' Then he bit his lip.

Riley Callaghan was actually nervous. It was the moment that she actually loved him most.

'I know it's soon. We can have a long engagement if you want. We can wait until after your surgery, and make sure that Finn is doing well, before we plan the wedding.' He squeezed her hand. 'But I want to let you know that this is it. This is it for me and Finn. We're yours, April Henderson. A package deal. And we'd like you to join our package. I love you, April. What do you say?'

She swallowed as a million thoughts swamped her head. Her heart so wanted to say yes. But she was still nervous.

'They think I'm clear, Riley. But what if I'm not? What if they find something—maybe not now, but later? What then, Riley? I don't want to put you in that position. I don't want to do that to you, or to Finn.'

Riley ran his fingers through his hair. 'How many times, April? How many times do you need me to tell you that I love you? That I accept the risks along with you. No one knows how long they have in this life. You don't know that, and neither do I. But I do know who I love, and who I want to spend the time I have on this earth with. That's you, April. It will only ever be you.'

She gulped as her eyes filled with tears.

He leaned his face close to hers. She could see every part of his green eyes. 'Tell me that you don't love me. Tell me that you don't love Finn. Tell me that you don't wonder about the life we could all have together.'

'Of course I do, Riley,' she whispered. She couldn't lie. Not when he was looking at her like that. Not when his love seemed to envelop every part of her.

He slid his hand into hers. 'We have a life. Let's live it, April. Let's live it together. You, me and Finn. This Christmas will be hard for Finn. But let's get through it together. You, me and him. Let's start something new. Let's create some memories together. As a family.'

She hesitated for the briefest of seconds as her heart swelled.

His eyes widened. 'Is that a yes?' Then he muttered under his breath, 'Please let that be a yes.'

She gave the surest nod she'd ever given. 'It's a yes,' she managed before his lips met hers.

EPILOGUE

IT HAD TAKEN HOURS, but Finn was finally sleeping. He'd crept back downstairs four times, asking if Santa had been yet, and each time Riley and April had laughed and chased him back upstairs.

But she'd just checked. He was now slightly snoring in bed, wearing his superhero onesie.

'At last,' groaned Riley as they flopped down on the sofa in front of the flickering fire. The tree with blue lights was in front of the main window, decorated with a mishmash of coloured baubles and topped with a golden star. April thought it was the most magnificent tree she'd ever seen. The decorations that they'd brought from Isabel's house had joined the new ones on the tree. It was just the way it should be—a mixture of the past and the present.

It had been a big day. She'd lived here since her discharge from hospital. Riley had insisted, and it had felt right. But today Finn had experienced a bit of a meltdown. She'd found him crying in the morning as the whole momentum of Christmas just seemed to overwhelm him. 'I miss my mum,' he'd whispered.

'I know, honey,' she'd said as she hugged him. 'I miss my sister too. But I think I know something we can do today that will help.'

Riley had been in complete agreement and they'd all gone shopping together in order to find something appropriate for Finn to take to his mother's grave. In the end he'd picked an ornament in the shape of a robin with a bright red breast. It was perfect. And they'd taken him to the cemetery and let him talk to his mother for a while and leave her the gift.

His mood had seemed easier after that, and April had gone and bought flowers to leave at her sister's grave too. 'We need to make this a tradition,' Riley had said quietly in her ear. 'Not a sad one for Christmas Eve, more like a chance to take five minutes to acknowledge the people who aren't here and are missed.'

And she agreed completely. It was something they would do together every year.

Now, it was finally time to relax. The presents were wrapped and under the tree, along with a tray with carrots, milk and mince pie for Santa. 'Better remember to eat that or there will be questions asked in the morning.'

April sighed. 'I've never been fond of carrots. Maybe we can hide it back in the fridge?'

Riley looked a bit odd. He stood up and walked over and picked up the little tray. 'I think Finn counted them earlier; we'd get found out.'

He sat back down on the sofa next to her and put the tray on her lap. He then knelt under the tree and added a couple of small red parcels. April tilted her head and looked at the tray. 'I think in future years, if I'm consuming what's on the tray for Santa, we'll have to negotiate its contents.'

'What does that mean?'

She grinned. 'It means that I think Santa might prefer a glass of wine and some chocolate cake.'

He nodded slowly. 'Why don't we just take things as they are right now?' He nudged her. 'Open your presents.'

She lifted the first one and tugged at the gold ribbon around the red glossy paper. She let out a gasp. It was the most perfect Christmas ornament she'd ever seen. A replica of her necklace. Two golden hearts joined together.

'Where on earth did you get this?' Her voice cracked slightly.

He smiled. 'I got it made for you. Do you like it?'

She nodded as she tried not to cry. 'I think it's perfect,' she sniffed.

He nudged her again. 'Open the next one.'

She smiled. 'I thought I was supposed to wait until Santa visited?'

He sighed. 'I'm far too impatient to wait for Santa.'

She pulled the ribbon on the second present. The paper fell away to reveal the church from the Christmas village. She felt her heart swell in her chest.

'I bought it for you after the Christmas Cheer Dinner. I wanted to remember how perfect that night was. And I thought we could add it to our collection.'

She hugged him. The way he said *our collection* just seemed perfect.

His face looked serious for a second. 'Now,

other traditions. It's time to eat the contents of the Christmas tray.'

She looked at him strangely and picked up the mince pie, taking a nibble. He kept watching her with those green eyes. When she finally finished she licked her fingers then picked up the carrot with her other hand. 'So what am I supposed to do with this?'

The carrot gave a wobble in mid-air then fell apart, one part bouncing onto the floor, the other part staying in her hand with something glistening at its core.

'What…?' she said as she turned it towards her.

She wasn't seeing things. There, somehow stuck inside the carrot, was a gold band and a rather large sparkly diamond. She turned back. Riley was sitting with the biggest grin on his face.

'Oh,' he said quickly. 'This is my cue to move.' And he did, moving off the sofa and onto the floor in front of her.

He took the carrot from her hand and gave the ring a little tug. 'Just so you know, the story is that Finn thinks Rudolph will leave the ring for you once he finds it.'

'He will?' She was mesmerised. She hadn't expected it at all. Sure, he'd called himself her fiancé in the hospital. But he'd talked about next year, after her surgery was completed, for making future plans.

Riley held it out towards her. The diamond caught the flickering light from the yellow flames of the fire, sending streams of light around the room. 'April, I love you with my whole heart. Even though you tried to avoid me, time and time again, I felt the pull from the first time we met. I know I haven't sorted out my job yet. I know we've still to get through your surgery. But I can't imagine a future with anyone but you. I don't *want* to have a future with anyone but you. I know it's soon. I know some people might think we are crazy. But will you marry us, April?'

Her heart gave a pitter-patter against her chest. Could she ask for any more?

She bent forward and slid her hands up around his neck. 'Now, this is what I call a proposal.'

He pulled her down onto his knee. 'Can I take that as a yes?'

She put her lips on his. 'You absolutely can.'

And there it was. The best Christmas *ever*.

* * * * *

LET'S TALK

Romance

For exclusive extracts, competitions
and special offers, find us online:

f facebook.com/millsandboon

⌾ @millsandboonuk

🐦 @millsandboon

Or get in touch on 0844 844 1351*

For all the latest titles coming soon,
visit millsandboon.co.uk/nextmonth

*Calls cost 7p per minute plus your phone company's price per
minute access charge

Want even more
ROMANCE?

Join our bookclub today!

Visit millsandbook.co.uk/Bookclub and save on brand new books.

MILLS & BOON